S0-AQP-722

*Mystery
at Snowshoe
Mountain
Lodge*

MRS. PECCHIA

MRS. PECCILIA

MYSTERY

—at— SNOWSHOE MOUNTAIN LODGE

Lisa Eisenberg

Troll Associates

A TROLL BOOK, published by Troll Associates,
Mahwah, NJ 07430

Copyright © 1987 by Lisa Eisenberg

All rights reserved. No part of this book may be reproduced or
utilized in any form or by any means, electronic or mechanical,
including photocopying, recording or by any storage and retrieval
system, without permission in writing from the Publisher.

Published by arrangement with Dial Books for Young Readers,
a division of NAL Penguin Inc. For information address
Dial Books for Young Readers, a division of NAL Penguin Inc.,
2 Park Avenue, New York, New York 10016.

First Troll Printing, 1988

Printed in the United States of America.

10 9 8 7 6 5 4 3 2 1

ISBN 0-8167-1322-7

To the real Ted, Kate, and Annie

*Mystery
at Snowshoe
Mountain
Lodge*

1

Sproing! The noisy, crowded bus bucked over a pothole, and my eyes shot open. I'd been right in the middle of a feverish nightmare, and for a few seconds I was so disoriented, I couldn't remember where I was. I turned my head and gaped groggily at two California-dream-type boys only a few feet away. They were total strangers. Still confused, I turned the other way and looked out a grimy window. What was all that snow doing out there? I've lived in Los Angeles my whole life long, and one thing I know for sure: It *never* snows in southern California!

The bus wheezed around a bend in the road, and I became aware that I was sitting at an extremely uncomfortable angle. My back and neck were hunched into the seat, and my knees were pointing straight up at the ceiling. We lurched over another bump, and suddenly I was jolted back into the real world. I was sitting at an angle because the nose of the bus was tilted upward, traveling along the winding pass to Snowshoe Mountain Lodge, high in the mountains of Utah. For the first time in my life I was going skiing.

Anxiously, I reached out for the small buttery-leather suitcase I'd placed on the empty seat next to me. Last night back in L.A., as I'd been stuffing sweaters, jeans, and wool socks into my dad's old army duffel bag, my mom had come into my room, gently cradling the suitcase. "Where did that come from?" I'd asked. I'd been sure I was acquainted with every ratty piece of luggage my family owns.

"Dad got it last year," my mother had said, stroking the tan side of the case. "He bought it for that trip to Hawaii, but then the company decided to have their sales convention right here in town. Before he left for Fresno this morning, he suggested I let you use the suitcase for your expedition."

With her busy, capable hands, Mom had pulled my messy clothes out of the duffel bag, folded them, and repacked them into the suitcase. "This is a special occasion," she'd gone on. "My little Kate's first trip on her own." She'd sounded like she was about to cry. You'd think I was four instead of fourteen!

"But I won't be on my own, Mom," I'd pointed out quickly. "Monty's going to be there!"

Monty is my first cousin and good friend, even though she's a year older than me and lives in Denver and we only get to see each other a few times a year. When I'd seen the notice about the skiing trip up on the bulletin board at school, I'd immediately thought of Monty. SKI SNOWSHOE! the sign had said. SIGN UP NOW FOR THE BEST SKIING IN THE WEST! The notice had gone on to say that one of the finest ski areas in Utah was offering very unusual bargain-basement package deals including room, board, lessons, and rental equipment for large school groups. The organizer, a boy in my class named Bobby Berman, was trying to get at least twenty kids from Pacifico to sign up so we could qualify for the deal.

Well, normally I wouldn't touch a ski slope with a ten-foot pole, but this trip sounded like a golden opportunity to get away from home on my own and miss a week of school. Several of my friends said they were going to sign up, so I called Monty and begged her to join us. My cousin has always loved skiing, and when I'd consulted Bobby, he'd said he thought there wouldn't be any problem about her signing on with our group even though she'd be coming from Colorado. Somehow, Monty managed to talk her father and mother, my Uncle Clark and Aunt Bea, into letting her go on the trip. Actually, I'd been quite surprised at how quickly she'd fallen in with my plans, since Monty always likes to be the one who arranges things. But as she said on the phone, Snowshoe Mountain has an international reputation and she'd always wanted to ski there.

To tell the truth, not long after we'd gotten the whole trip arranged, I'd tried to back out. First of all, after convincing me to come along, every single one of my Pacifico friends had come up with an excuse for not going after all, so I was faced with traveling with a bunch of kids I barely knew. Second, as the day of the trip had approached, I'd started having nightmares about making a total fool of myself learning how to ski. In a panic, I'd gone to Bobby Berman and begged for my deposit back, but he'd said it was "nonrefundable." And then my parents had come up with this thing about how this trip would help me become more independent, and how I'd made a commitment to Monty and now I had to honor it. And finally Monty had said that if I backed out of the trip, she personally would fly to California and break every bone in my body for me!

So here I was, miles away from home, alone in a crowd of kids who barely acknowledged my existence. As everyone on the bus chattered about ski equipment and snow conditions, I secretly plotted ways and means of avoiding skiing altogether. I've never cared much for athletics. I also don't particularly like trying new things, being brave, and making the best of a bad situation. Why, why had I let my fickle friends talk me into this trip?

With a great mental effort I told myself to look on the bright side. While the actual skiing might be a problem, I argued, I could surely find happiness in buying new sweaters at the ski shop, lounging around a roaring fire, guzzling hot chocolate, and flirting with all the Swiss ski instructors. And Monty and I always had a lot of fun with no parents around. We could stay up as late as we wanted, and even eat candy in bed. My mom is basically all right, but she has an unnatural obsession with dental hygiene. A person can't even mention a Snickers bar in our house.

Thinking of food made me feel hungry, a very common reaction with me. Hopefully, I started digging around in my jacket pocket, praying that by some miracle I'd left a few comforting peanut M&M's in the bag I'd bought in the bus station when my mom was in the ladies' room. Of course, I only found the crumpled-up yellow wrapper. I stared out the window again and saw that we were climbing up through a forest of tall, elegant-looking pine trees. It was amazing how, in just a few minutes, we'd gone from the hot Utah flatlands to this alpine scene right out of *The Sound of Music.*

I opened the side flap of my dad's suitcase and pulled out the book I'd brought along with me. It was a scary new Oliver Strangeway novel that Monty had sent me for my birthday. It was called *House of Unspeakable Evil,* and on the cover was a picture of a creepy old house with a skeleton looking out of one window. As I stared at the two bloated, gory rats creeping out of the skeleton's eye sockets, I shuddered.

Reluctantly, I turned to the first page and started to read. Within a few hair-raising sentences, however, I closed the book and hastily stuffed it back into my suitcase. Normally I love terrifying myself with a gross horror story, but today my stomach already had enough on its mind what with worrying about things like missing my parents, traveling alone, and dreading ski lessons. Besides, the ride from Los Angeles had taken many long hours so far, and my neck felt too stiff and tired to hold my head up. I closed my eyes and tried to use mental telepathy to make the bus go faster.

"Hey, Clancy!" a voice called from the aisle. "Could you move your suitcase so I can sit down?"

If I kept my eyes closed and pretended to still be asleep, maybe he'd go away. Of course, I recognized the voice at once. It was Bobby "Mouth" Berman, himself, the organizer of this trip and the biggest loudmouth at Pacifico High. At one point, when he'd been so cooperative about letting Monty join our group, I'd been on the verge of thinking Bobby wasn't such a bad guy. But when he'd been so mean about refunding my deposit, I'd decided to have nothing more to do with him ever again.

If he insisted on sitting by me, it would be hard to keep to that decision. What in the world did he need a seat for now, when the trip was almost over? As soon as I asked myself the question, the answer came to me with dreary certainty. Obviously, the person Mouth had been sitting next to for all those unbearable hours had finally gone berserk and kicked him into the aisle.

Now Bobby was hauling and tugging at my suitcase, trying to move it himself. Without looking at him, I sighed, got to my feet, and hoisted the luggage onto the overhead rack. Bobby made a move to sit down, but all at once he toppled forward and crashed over right onto my lap. I screamed, and half the people on the bus nearly broke their necks twisting their heads around to stare at us. I felt myself turning bright red.

"Get off me!" I snarled. Bobby flailed his arms, searching for something to grab onto to pull himself up. I couldn't stand it anymore. I took hold of both his shoulders and gave a mighty sideways heave. Bobby fell off my lap and slid down into a folded-up position, wedged between my knees and the back of the seat in front of us. For a tense moment I thought he was really stuck there and that they'd have to call in a welder with an acetylene blowtorch to blast us out of the bus. Finally, though, with a lot of grunting and groaning, he managed to wriggle sideways and upward into the empty aisle seat.

"Sorry about that, Clancy," he gasped. "I'm not used to walking around in these things."

I looked down at Bobby's feet and saw that they were already buckled up into a pair of gargantuan orange ski boots. He looked like some kind of overweight astronaut. "Why are you wearing those now?" I asked. "I thought they were only for skiing."

"They're molding themselves to the shape of my feet," Bobby explained. "So they'll be a perfect fit when I hit the slopes tomorrow. Comfortable equipment is an absolute must."

Bobby always talked about skiing as if he were about to turn pro, but I secretly wondered if he could really be as good as he said. As he blathered away, I gazed out the window, with my forehead knocking against the glass whenever the driver scored a bull's-eye with another pothole. I wondered if this crummy little road was the only way to get up or down the mountain. A really good snowstorm could cut us off completely.

"How much farther till we get there?" I asked Bobby.

"Oh, it won't be much farther now, Clance." Bobby pointed out the window. "There's Clementine's Hotel. That's the ski area on Sunburst Mountain. It's not bad. Though the really good people usually go on up the road to Snowshoe. That is . . . before mutsputsflix . . ."

His voice trailed off, and he muttered something else I couldn't quite catch. As you might imagine, with Mouth Berman muttering is almost unheard of. I turned sideways and stared at him in surprise. "What's that you said, Bobby?"

"Oh, nothing," he answered. "I was just talking to myself."

"Come on, Bobby," I said. "You started to say 'before' something. Before what?"

"It's nothing, I said, Clancy. Just some stupid story I heard from some friends of mine who went skiing at Snowshoe last month."

I waited for him to go on, but once again he was abnormally quiet. "What did they say?" I asked at last.

"What did who say?"

"Your friends, of course! The ones who went skiing! What did they say about Snowshoe Mountain?" My voice was starting to sound pretty whiny, but I couldn't help myself.

"Oh, that," Bobby said with elaborate casualness. "It's really too dumb to repeat. Something about a legend. I don't even remember what it was all about." He bent down and fiddled with his ski boot.

"Oh, come on," I said again. "What is it?"

"What is what?" Bobby asked without sitting up. He turned his attention to his other boot, and I gazed down at his neck with murder in my heart. If I'd strangled him, I'm sure any judge and jury in the country would have said it was justifiable homicide. But then I never would have heard the story. "What did your friends tell you about a legend?" I asked through clenched teeth.

Bobby sat up and cast a furtive look around the bus. "Well . . . all right, I'll tell you, Clancy, since you're obviously going to have a nervous breakdown if I don't. But remember, I said it was dumb." He cleared his throat and moved his mouth close to my ear. "My friends said there were some strange things happening in the lodge . . . and a story going around . . . about an old legend . . . that said . . . the place was . . . well, that it was haunted."

My first instinct was to laugh. "You're kidding!" I chortled. "Are your friends lunatics, or what?"

I was sure Bobby would start laughing right along with me, but to my surprise he remained serious. "I thought they were joking myself," he answered thoughtfully. "But you should have heard them talk about the place. They said things vanished into thin air. They saw mysterious moving lights on the mountainside in the middle of the night. They heard creaky floorboards behind them in the hallways when no one was there. And after all, Clancy, you don't know what a ski lodge is like. You're all alone up there on a cold, blowy mountainside, completely cut off from civilization. Almost anything could happen in a creepy situation like that. My friends weren't the only ones who got scared off."

I stared into Bobby's eyes. A cold chill ran up and down my spine, and it took tremendous willpower for me to answer him in my best sneering, incredulous voice. "You're sure your friends were serious when they told you all this?"

"Oh, they were serious all right. They came back from their trip a week early! And they tried to convince me not to come up here. Of course," Bobby added quickly, "I didn't listen."

A small voice inside my head let out a long groan. All at once I couldn't bear to continue the conversation. I shrugged, shook my head in amused disbelief, and then pretended an intense, renewed interest in the view outside the window.

Fantastic, I told myself. Now, on top of all my other anxieties, I would have to worry about the stupid lodge being haunted! I tried to reassure myself with the thought that any friends of Mouth Berman's were bound to be total morons, but somehow it didn't help much. I had a sudden, vivid image of myself lying flat on my back while a ghastly, clammy apparition clawed at my hair. I was struggling to escape, but I was immobilized by my broken leg, which was suspended from a giant pulley over the bed. And then the thought of broken bones reminded me of something else Mouth had said.

I turned away from the window. "Bobby," I said, "you said the really good skiers all go up to ski at Snowshoe instead of staying down at Clementine's. Does that mean the trails at Snowshoe are the hardest?"

Suddenly, Mouth was back in his old form. He laughed so loud that heads on the bus started twisting around again. "Don't worry, Clancy," he boomed. "There'll be plenty of baby trails for you to fall down."

The two boys across the aisle looked at each other and smirked. With my luck they'd probably concluded that Mouth was my boyfriend. As I brooded about that, the bus pulled into a large, snowy parking lot and groaned to a stop. I peered out the window. Directly before my eyes was a wide expanse of white, dotted with tiny moving black spots. It looked like a steep, brilliant wall of snow rising straight up into the blue sky.

"What's that?" I asked Bobby.

"Oh, that," he boomed. "That's the beginners' slope, Clancy. Around here they call it Deadman's Run!"

2

For a few hideous seconds I was dumb enough to believe Bobby. Then I realized he was roaring with laughter again, along with everyone else on the bus. With what little dignity I could muster, I got to my feet, retrieved my suitcase from the overhead rack, and marched off the bus.

Outside in the parking lot, the glare from the sun bounced off the snow and made me temporarily blind. When the purple spots faded, I looked up and saw Snowshoe Mountain Lodge. I'd always thought that ski lodges had to be modern and triangular, with glass walls and pointed wooden roofs. But this place was nothing like that. It was old, and sort of castlelike, made of gray stone with two round tower rooms sticking up and billions of oddly shaped gables. There were large, black picture windows on either side of the double wooden front doors. Call me overimaginative if you want, but to me those windows looked exactly like a pair of enormous, unblinking, hostile eyes, watching me. Silently daring me to come closer.

For some reason the place looked strangely familiar, and suddenly I realized why. It was almost a dead ringer for the spooky mansion on the cover of *House of Unspeakable Evil*. I glanced over my shoulder to see how the other passengers were reacting to this obviously weird place. To my surprise no one else seemed to be paying much attention. Most of the people were hauling their luggage off the bus and straggling over toward some wooden steps that led up out of the parking lot. At the top they followed an icy path to the hotel, where they passed through the two gigantic mahogany doors.

I stood still for a minute, trying to shake off my feeling of uneasiness. I decided I had no choice but to follow the rest of the crowd. I picked up Dad's suitcase and headed for the wooden steps. I slipped and slid up the rickety stairs, wondering why no one had cleared away the treacherous ice.

As I approached the front doors, I almost expected to see them creak inward on their own power. Instead they burst open, and a very short, red-haired girl with pigtails bounced out and almost slipped on a patch of ice. At first I thought she'd been crying, because her eyes were all red. But then I saw that her nose was also a vivid scarlet and that she was carrying a wad of green tissues in one hand. She waved the clipboard and started to speak to me, but then stopped and sneezed loudly instead.

"I hab the worst code," she told me, frowning down at the path. "Gosh. How did all this ice ged here? I know Peter shoveled this walk just last dight. Or at least Lars told me he did. . . ." Her perky face assumed an oddly worried expression, and she seemed to be lost in thought. I put down my suitcase, cleared my throat, and told her who I was.

"Kate Clancy," she repeated, hastily coming back to

the present. She ran her pencil down the list. "Oh, here you are! Welcobe to Snowshoe Bountain. I'b Pixie Henderson, the acting head of the ski school."

I stared in disbelief. Of course, I'd noticed that Pixie Henderson was wearing a green-and-white jumpsuit uniform with a big snowshoe on the sleeve, but I'd assumed she was a junior kitchen trainee or something. I mean, I've already mentioned how little and short she was. And she didn't look old enough to be away from home, let alone the acting head of the ski school.

She scratched her bright head with her pencil. "Kate Clancy," she said again. "I think there was a message for you at the front desk. Some kind of problem came up. Anyway, you have to check in there to get your room key. I'll see you later, at didder. We eat family style here, starting at six o'clock."

I hurried into the lodge, wondering what my message could possibly be. Pixie had said there was some kind of problem. Could something be wrong at home already?

I was so sure tragedy had struck that I barely noticed what the inside of the lodge looked like. As I dashed across the lobby, I was vaguely aware of a groaning wood floor and some large, heavy pieces of old-fashioned furniture. I spotted a small, middle-aged woman sitting behind a reception desk. She seemed to be arguing with a gray-haired, nervous-looking man and his gray-haired, jumpy-looking wife. I scurried over in their direction and arrived at the desk just in time to watch the man give a nervous start and say something that sounded like "midnight dreary," quickly followed by the phrase "full refund."

The man and woman stalked away. Too distracted to wonder what their problem was, I practically threw myself across the top of the desk. "I'm Kate Clancy," I gasped. "What's happened?"

The woman behind the desk didn't even appear to notice me. She was breathing quickly and struggling to open the top of a little bottle. As she twisted and clawed at the lid, two tiny charms on a gold chain tinkled on her wrist. When she had finally managed to wrestle the lid off the bottle, she poured three yellow pills into her hand and greedily gulped them down. She took a long swallow from a water glass sitting on the desk. At last she looked up at me, suddenly seeming to realize I'd spoken to her.

"Can I help you?" she asked. She spoke with a heavy French accent, and it seemed to be a great effort for her to force the words out of her mouth. She had an outdoorsy kind of face, weathered and tan, and around her eyes were tiny, attractive lines, as if she was someone who liked to smile a lot. She certainly wasn't smiling now.

"I'm Kate Clancy," I said again. "I was told there was a message for me."

The woman stared at me, struggling to get me into focus. "A message?" she said vaguely. "From whom?"

"How should I know?" I said impatiently. "I just got here!"

The woman blinked and ran a hand over her hair. She

looked up and tried to rearrange her face into a smile. "I think we need to start over, you and I," she said. "You must think I have gone crazy. And perhaps you are right!" She started to laugh and then stopped abruptly. She held out her hand. As she clasped my fingers in a firm grip, I had a sudden image of a warm, friendly person trapped inside a tangled web of frayed nerves. "I am Camille Higonnet, the owner of the lodge," she said. "And I believe you said your name is Kate Clancy?"

She began thumbing through a pile of pink paper slips on her desk, and her bracelets began their delicate music again. "Ah, here it is. Let me see. Your cousin Monty called. It seems she is sick and her father won't let her come skiing after all."

I glanced over at the woman, trying to convince myself that she might have hallucinated my message. But she was giving me such a sympathetic look that I decided I had to face the grim facts. No matter how you looked at it, Monty was the only reason I'd come on this trip. And now she wasn't coming. I was all alone in this creepy lodge with nothing to live for but the chance of breaking my neck on the ski slopes. All at once I knew I was going to cry.

Then I had an idea. "The bus," I croaked out. "If it's still here, I can get back on it. I'll go back home tonight."

The lodge owner's tired eyes were apologetic. "I'm sorry," she said. "But that is impossible. The bus isn't going back to Los Angeles until late tomorrow. I'm afraid you must stay with us for at least one night and day."

I blinked my eyes and turned my head in a desperate attempt to keep the tears from falling. Just then I noticed a tall, black-haired boy slouching against the wall nearby, outside a door labeled OFFICE. He appeared to be about seventeen or so, and was dressed in a black shirt, black slacks, and a shiny black-leather fringed vest. He was devastatingly handsome, particularly if you go for the dark, sullen type.

He looked as if he was brooding about something, but when he saw me notice him, he gave a half smile and walked over to us. As he approached, I saw he had a tool belt slung around his narrow waist. When he moved, the tools on the belt *clickety-clack*ed into one another.

"I couldn't help hearing about your problem," he said in a low, smooth voice. "That's rough luck. But you really shouldn't feel so bad. Lots of people come here alone, but they make friends in their ski classes. It's hard *not* to make friends with people who are falling down the mountainside with you!"

He gave a surprisingly deep chuckle, and in spite of myself I laughed too. The boy was looking straight at me with a pair of shadowy, almost-black eyes. As I gazed at him, I noticed that instead of two eyebrows, he actually only had one giant one that went across his entire forehead. On anyone else it might have looked sort of sinister, but for some reason on him it was very attractive.

Ms. Higonnet came around the desk and put a petite hand on the boy's arm. I realized that, like Pixie and unlike me, she was tiny and delicate. "This is Peter Shade,

Kate," the woman said. "He is the son of our bookkeeper, Marsha, and has lived in this area all his life. He is the part-time lodge handyman, but is also teaching in the ski school during his winter vacation. If you are lucky, you will be in his class tomorrow."

Peter Shade, I thought. What a romantic name. Maybe it might be worth sticking around for a while and trying my hand, or feet, at a few skiing lessons. If I hated it, I could always get on the bus when it finally did go back to L.A.

Peter told me he had to go teach a private lesson, but added that he hoped he'd see me around. As he left, I watched him take off his tool belt and hang it on a hook on the side of the check-in desk. Then I saw that Ms. Higonnet was searching through some keys hanging on hooks on the wall behind her. "Mixed up again," she was muttering to herself. "And the desk has not been left un-guarded all day."

She suddenly became aware I was eavesdropping on this strange monologue, and she immediately stopped talking to herself. "Ah," she said in her normal voice, "here is the key I was seeking. We've put you in room thirteen in the east wing. Go up the three steps, through the doors, down the hall, and turn left at the first corner."

"Thank you, Ms. Higonnet," I said, taking the key.

"Oh, call me Camille," she said. "Everyone does. That is, those people who are still speaking to me." She gave an odd kind of half laugh, half cry, and quickly covered her mouth with her hand. Good grief, I thought. Crack-Up

City, U.S.A. But what a pity it had to happen to such a nice person.

I started toward the steps, but stopped when I saw Pixie coming in my direction, carrying my suitcase. "You forgot this outside," she said through her nose. "It's such a nice one, I was sure you wouldn't want to lose it!"

"Oh, thanks, Pixie," I said gratefully. "It's my dad's, so I have to be specially careful with it." I couldn't believe I'd been so careless with my precious luggage! Maybe *I* was cracking up now.

Pixie smiled, sneezed, and bounced back to her station outside the front doors. I bent down to brush off a few globs of dirty snow some sloppy skier had kicked onto the suitcase.

"Hi, Kathy. I didn't know you were on this trip."

I glanced up and gave a start of surprise. Standing, or should I say posing, above me was Lynda Dalton, a stunning blond schoolmate of mine from Pacifico. I was surprised for two reasons: first, that I hadn't noticed her on the bus; second, that Lynda, even though she'd gotten my name wrong, was condescending to speak to me at all.

Her ulterior motive soon became clear. "I hope we'll end up in the same class tomorrow, Kath," she said. "By the way, I saw you talking to that awesome-looking mystery man with the tool belt over there by the desk. Is he a friend of yours? Do you think you could introduce us?"

I pretended to still be absorbed in cleaning my suitcase. Then I looked into Lynda's huge, heavily made up, bright-blue eyes. "You'll have to introduce yourself, *Lydia,*" I muttered at last. "I hardly know that boy." And, I thought bitterly, now that you're here, it looks like I never will.

3

As I crept along the narrow, shadowy halls in search of Room 13, I couldn't help but wonder about the lunatic who'd designed such a bizarro building for a ski lodge. Where were the wooden beams and Swedish fireplaces I'd always seen in the movies? This place seemed more like a retreat for an eccentric madman. On top of that I had the strangest sensation of not being really alone. Of being watched, somehow. Involuntarily, I thought of Bobby Berman's friends' weird stories about groans and lights and vanishing objects. Was I already succumbing to the creepy atmosphere?

I'd just about given myself up for lost when I ran into Bobby himself, wandering around with a big key with the number 14 on it. It seemed that if we ever found our rooms, we would be next-door neighbors. At last, after several wrong turns, we stumbled onto the right hall. Fortunately, my room turned out to be nicer than I'd dared to hope. Given what I'd seen of the lodge so far, I'd been expecting something along the lines of a dank dungeon complete with spiders and moldy bread crusts. Instead, Room 13 had two double beds, rag rugs, and a comfortable old chintz rocking chair. One wall was almost entirely taken up with a huge, old-fashioned wardrobe. In the corner stood a large television set, with cable and HBO. Mournfully, I thought of the fun Monty and I would have had watching it.

I lifted Dad's suitcase onto one of the patchwork-quilted beds and halfheartedly started unpacking. But after I took out my nightgown and toothbrush, I was irresistibly drawn to the window. I pulled back the heavy curtain and gasped. In the late-afternoon light, Snowshoe Mountain cast long, twisted dark purple shadows. The only ski slope I could see was empty, except for one girl gliding down the wide trail. Her motions were so fluid and graceful, it almost looked as if she weren't even touching the ground. Come to think of it, maybe she *wasn't* touching the ground! Maybe she was a ghost, out for one last run before she had to report for haunting duty.

The idea of a ghost having to punch a time clock and report to a ghost foreman for her evening assignment struck me as hilarious, and I gave a high-pitched laugh. Then I had a sudden vision of myself, standing all alone in my room, shrieking like mad Bertha in *Jane Eyre* (my all-time favorite book), and I quickly cut myself off in mid cackle. At this rate I'd be out in the lobby in a minute, swilling tranquilizers with Camille Higonnet. Be rational, I told myself. The girl outside was simply a very good

23

skier. With debonair Peter Shade's help (I fervently hoped), I'd undoubtedly be skiing just like her by tomorrow afternoon.

I watched the skier pass behind some small, modern-looking cottages behind the main lodge, and then she skied out of my range of vision. I started away from the window, but a movement outside caught my eye. With my face pressed up against the cold glass, I gazed out at the deserted ski slope. Had something actually moved out there, or had it just been a clawlike, leafless branch shifting in the wind? I could have sworn I'd seen a sort of barrel-shaped dark figure stealthily glide into the black shadows beneath my window. But after I'd stared out at the snow for a few minutes, I decided my imagination was playing a practical joke on me.

To calm myself down, I went to the bathroom to throw cold water on my face and stare at my reflection in the mirror (always a sobering experience). As usual, my long brown hair was standing out in a fuzzy bush around my head. I gazed at my eyes, wondering if I should start using more shadow and mascara, like Lynda Dalton. It certainly looked good on her, but then she had huge, round blue eyes instead of almond-shaped, sleepy-looking gray ones like mine.

I sighed, splashed some more water on my cheeks, and toweled off. Back out in the room, I found a full-length mirror inside the door of the big wardrobe. I looked at myself in my baggy old red sweater and faded jeans, wondering if I should change for dinner. At last I decided that no matter what I wore, my skinny body would never look like Lynda Dalton's. I found the room key, went out into the hall, and locked my door.

Unfortunately, I was born with almost no sense of direction whatsoever, so I couldn't rely on my instincts to get me back to civilization. I tried to use the other room numbers as clues, but there didn't seem to be any system to the way they were arranged, and it occurred to me that the brass numerals on the doors were as mixed up as the keys out by the front desk. For some reason the halls were completely empty, so I couldn't even discreetly tag along behind any of the other guests. Maybe there weren't any other guests left. Maybe I was the only human being left in the hotel.

Stop it! I screamed to myself. Stop behaving like a total idiot. I hurried forward, desperate for any form of companionship, so long as it was human. I went around a bend in the hall, and there were the lights of the lobby. I was about to kiss the floorboards when I realized I wasn't alone. Petite Camille Higonnet and a tall, gray-haired woman were huddled together in the shadows just beyond the arched entrance to the lobby, having a very intense whispered conversation. As I approached, the floor creaked, and the two women quickly broke apart and moved into the lobby. Just before the pair split up, I was almost positive I heard the tall woman hiss out the word "menace!"

It was disturbing but I didn't have much time to ponder it, because just then five cool, strong fingers gripped my elbow from behind. I gasped and staggered forward, awkwardly banging my shoulder against the wall. I wrenched around and looked directly into Peter Shade's magnetic black eyes.

"I'm sorry, Kate," he said in his low voice. "I didn't mean to startle you. I was just going into the dining room when I saw you standing here, and I wondered if you'd let me take you in to dinner."

I was so mesmerized by his gaze that it didn't occur to me to wonder if he'd observed the weird scene between Camille and the gray-haired woman, or to ask how he could possibly have noticed me on his way into the dining room when he'd just come up *behind* me in the dark hallway. With his hand still on my elbow, Peter guided me through the arched entrance to the dining room, a dimly lit, high-ceilinged cavern just off the lobby, and found us seats at one of the round wooden tables that filled the room. I had the feeling he was about to ask me something when Pixie Henderson and a strong-looking, suntanned, surfer-blond man came in and sat down right next to us. The man was wearing the same type of green-and-white-colored jumpsuit as Pixie, so I figured he also had to be on the lodge staff. They both looked cold, as if they'd just been outside, and Peter explained that most of the ski instructors lived in the little cottages I'd noticed behind the main lodge.

Pixie sneezed, blew her nose, and then gave me a watery smile. "Hi, Kate," she said. "Hi, Peter." She waved a hand (and a fluttering green tissue) toward the blond man.

"This is Lars Lundquist. He's our newest instructor in the ski school. He came here last ski season from Sweden."

The man leaned over and gave me a little bow. When he did, two small, gold medallions around his neck bonked into each other with a pleasant clicking sound. "It is a pleasure to meet you, Kate," he said. His accent sounded just like Mrs. Olson's in the coffee commercials, and I immediately decided he was almost as good-looking as Peter Shade, though they were complete opposites. Where Peter's hair was dark and smooth, Lars's was blond and shaggy. And where Peter's eyes were that hypnotic near black, Lars's were a clear, piercing ice blue. In fact, they were such an unusual shade of blue, I couldn't help staring at them. As I did, I noticed one of them twitch slightly in one corner. At first I thought Lars might be winking at me, but the truth was that he wasn't even looking in my direction when it happened.

Lars wasn't looking at me because, like everyone else, he was looking at the doorway where, at that instant, Lynda Dalton was making her entrance into the dining room. For a long moment she stood poised in front of us, casually tossing her shiny blond hair this way and that as she surveyed the roomful of people. She was now wearing an expensive-looking deep-green sweater, and ski pants of the same color.

Just then her glance fell on Peter, and she went into immediate action. Ignoring several tables filled with her best friends from Pacifico, she shot across the room and sat down right next to me. "Hi, Kathy," she said, giving me a little squeeze.

Pixie looked dismayed. "Oh, I'm sorry, Kathy," she said. "I've been calling you Kate. You should have corrected me."

"It *is* Kate," I mumbled, turning a bright shade of red. With a pretty little wave of her hand, Lynda introduced herself. Then she turned to Peter and began a long, meaningful conversation about the importance of skiing in her life.

Soon Camille and several waiters and waitresses began bringing big platters around to all the tables. The food looked great. Tiny, juicy stuffed hens were surrounded by piles of delicately cut French fried potatoes. Even the buttery vegetables, which I normally loathe, looked mouthwatering. Pixie and Lars explained that Camille supervised everything in the kitchen and even helped out with some of the cooking, in addition to managing the hotel and teaching skiing. I was impressed, but also puzzled. How did all this capability and competence fit in with the obviously disturbed woman I'd met in the lobby?

"How long has Camille owned this place, anyway?" I asked.

"She inherited it from an uncle about a year ago," Pixie answered, muffling a sneeze. "I know exactly, because it was my fifth anniversary working in the ski school here." She dabbed at her poor nose and took a bite of peas. "Also, that's when things began to—Gosh!" she interrupted herself. "These vegetables are salty!" she exclaimed. "I wonder if—"

"They taste fine to me," Peter Shade broke in. His voice was so sharp that I turned to stare at him in surprise. When I glanced back at Pixie, she had an embarrassed expression on her face. What's going on around here? I asked myself. I'd been planning to ask Pixie about Bobby's friends' spooky stories, but now I decided not to. She probably wouldn't tell me anything anyway, I thought. There seemed to be some kind of conspiracy of silence going on in this place. But silence about what?

As I pondered my little mystery, a loud commotion sounded from the direction of the lobby. Across the room I saw Camille turn pale and put a shaking hand to her lips. Then she got out of her seat and started toward the door. But before she'd taken more than two steps, Bobby "Mouth" Berman marched into the room. He was wearing the same clothes he'd worn on the bus, except that he was in his stocking feet. In each hand he held a giant orange ski boot. "How did this happen?" he bellowed. "Who filled my new ski boots with snow and put them outside my window? They're half frozen. And completely ruined!"

It might have been funny. But no one looked the slightest bit amused. Red-nosed Pixie was staring across the table at shaggy-haired Lars, who was staring at his hands and fiddling with his medallions while his right eye twitched uncontrollably. Lynda Dalton was staring at Peter Shade, who in turn was staring at someone in the far corner of the room whom I couldn't see. Camille was standing by her table, staring at the floor like she was about to fall right over on her face.

What about me? Well, I was still staring at Bobby. But I wasn't really seeing him. Instead I was recalling the dark figure I thought I'd imagined lurking around in the shadows outside my window. And I was remembering that Bobby's room was right next door to mine.

4

Camille stood where she was, white as a ghost, swaying on her feet and wringing her hands. She looked so ghastly, I was sure we were going to have to call in the paramedics to revive her. Finally, though, she gave a low, gasping moan and seemed to pull herself together. She crossed the room to Bobby's side and led him out into the lobby. A few minutes later she brought him back into the dining room and right over to our table.

"I just can't understand it," Bobby said as he ate. "I took my boots off and went into the shower, and when I came back out half an hour later, the boots were on the ledge outside my window, full of water. But my door was still locked *with the safety chain on!*"

Pixie gave a loud gasp of dismay, and I noticed that Bobby's face was much paler than its usual beet red. Once again I thought of the spooky figure moving around in the snow outside our rooms. "Did you check to see if your window was open, Bobby?" I asked.

"Of course I did, Clancy," he said. Was his voice a little shaky? "And *it* was locked from the inside also! I even went out and searched up and down all the halls for a secret entrance or some kind of device that might have unlocked the safety chain from the outside, but I couldn't find a thing."

He took a bite of bread and went on talking in his regular voice. "Camille says she thinks she can get my boots dried out so I can use them in a day or two. And in the meantime she's letting me pick out a new pair of boots from the ski shop. She says they stock the same brand that I have."

Well, Lars's eye had temporarily stopped twitching and Pixie's nose had temporarily stopped sniffling, so now Bobby and the two ski instructors were able to concentrate on a technical (translate that as boring) discussion of the pros and cons of different types of ski boots. To my astonishment Pixie and Lars listened to Bobby with genuine interest. Could it be that he actually knew what he was talking about?

I was sure that Peter would have had something insightful to say about ski boots if Lynda had given him a chance to talk to anyone else at the table. But she kept him completely occupied, plying him with questions about skiing. At one point I overheard her asking him if he had time to give her a private lesson tomorrow so she could work on the fine points of her technique. After that I tried not to listen. Besides, my mind was busy with trying to solve the "locked room" mystery Bobby had just presented to us.

I didn't make much progress with the puzzle, but I forgot about it when dessert showed up. It almost made up for everything else that had gone wrong that day, and that is really saying something! It was raspberry shortcake with fresh strawberries and real whipped cream. As we were finishing up the dessert, Pixie mentioned that, after dinner, an old Fred Astaire movie was being shown in the front parlor. Like a fool, I blurted out that I was a big fan of Fred Astaire's. Before I knew it, Bobby asked me to go to the movie with him.

Oh, dear. Why did he have to ask me right in front of Peter Shade? I was caught in a real no-win situation. If I said yes, I'd be paired up with loudmouth Bobby. But if I said no, I'd look like a real witch.

Frantically, I ransacked my brain for some kind of plausible excuse for skipping the movie. Within seconds, however, I knew I had to accept my fate. I decided to put a good face on things. "Sure, Mouth . . . er, Bobby," I said brightly. "That sounds like fun."

And actually it wasn't that bad. Of course, Bobby talked too much and too loud, but some of what he had to say was really interesting. Before the movie started, he gave me a lot of advice about how to handle my first day on skis, telling me that even though it would probably seem impossible at first, things really would get easier after a few lessons. I took all this compassion as a kind of apology for the way he'd humiliated me on the bus. He also asked if I'd like him to take me down to the rental shop after breakfast the next morning and help me get fitted for skis and boots. I was glad to accept this offer, since I didn't have a clue about what kind of equipment I'd be needing and was sure I'd ask for the wrong thing. As the lights went off, I realized that my opinions about Bobby had begun to change. To my surprise, I discovered I was actually glad I'd told him I'd come to the movie with him!

In fact, Bobby was being so nice that I began to think I owed it to him to tell him about the mysterious moving shadow outside our rooms. But I still wasn't sure he wouldn't laugh at me, and as you may have noticed, when Bobby Berman laughs, the whole world listens. Besides, the rational part of my brain kept on telling me I'd only imagined the figure on the snow. Of course, that still didn't explain how someone (or some*thing,* as they say in scary books) had gotten in and out of Bobby's locked room.

When the movie started, I settled down to watch but for once I couldn't get involved in what was happening on the screen. The events of the day were so weird, I had trouble thinking of anything else. When the lights came back on, I blinked in surprise, and realized I'd completely missed seeing Fred and Ginger dance the Piccolino.

I got up and looked around—and was maliciously delighted to see Lynda Dalton sitting all by herself on a folding chair in a corner. Then I saw that Peter was at the back of the room, rewinding the film on the projector.

As I discreetly watched him, I realized he was discreetly watching someone else. When I followed the path of his gaze to the other side of the room, I recognized the tall, gray-haired woman I'd seen huddled in the shadows with Camille right before dinner. She was bustling around the parlor, folding up chairs and putting them away.

When the woman came in my direction, I got a good look at her face and realized she *had* to be the lodge book-keeper, Marsha Shade, Peter's mother. She had almost the exact same black eyes as her son. The only difference was that hers were ringed with dark circles of fatigue.

But, I asked myself, if this woman was Peter's mother, why was Peter looking at her like that? His expression was hard to describe, sort of an alarming combination of speculation and controlled fury. But even as I continued to watch the pair, Peter's mother glanced anxiously in his direction, and his expression immediately went blank.

After that, Bobby and I walked back toward our rooms. When we came to Room 14, I stuck my head in long enough to observe that it was almost an exact duplicate of my own, with double beds, big wardrobe, chintz rocking chair, etc. Then I told Bobby good night and promised to see him right after breakfast.

Back in my own room, I closed the door and put on the safety chain. Suddenly I realized that, while my body was completely exhausted, my brain was going a mile a milli-second, trying to make some kind of sense out of all the crazy things that had happened during the day. I sank down into the chintz rocker and started rocking back and forth, to an accompaniment of groans from the old chair. The weirdest thing, I decided at last, was that aside from the creepy building and general sinister atmosphere of gloom, there was something odd about practically everyone associated with the lodge.

Why were they like that? Was the strain of living in this isolated place under the cloud of a ghostly legend beginning to tell on all of them? After a few days here would I be acting as wacko as they were, seeing moving lights, hearing groans, biting my nails, and staring angrily off into space? Was that why the room was slowly spinning around and my eyelids were being dragged down by heavy chains and . . . *Whoa!* Suddenly I realized I was falling asleep sitting up. I decided to crawl into bed and forget all this confusing nonsense till tomorrow. I couldn't face the job of unpacking, even though Mom always says to do it right away so my clothes won't wrinkle. Guiltily, I stood up . . . took my father's precious suitcase off Monty's empty bed, and stuffed it into my seat on the chintz rocking chair, where I wouldn't be able to see it from my bed.

Drowsily, I pulled on my favorite old flannel night-gown, brushed and flossed in the bathroom, and climbed under the covers. Out of force of habit, as I passed the rocker I took a book out of the flap of my suitcase so I could read myself to sleep, but I didn't even make it to the end of the first page of *House of Unspeakable Evil*. In about half a second I started drifting off with the open book on my chest. One hand automatically reached out and switched off the bedside lamp. Then I was totally lost to the world, having my usual recurring bad dream about showing up for an algebra test without my socks or my teeth.

I have no idea how long I'd been asleep when I woke up with my heart wildly thumping against the inside of my rib cage. I gave one violent lurch of surprise, and *House of Unspeakable Evil* toppled off my chest and landed on the floor with a thump. As I slid my trembling body down under the quilt, I heard it again. It was a muffled noise only a few feet away from the bed. I couldn't figure out what the sound was, only that it was somehow vaguely familiar. And that it meant someone (or something) was in my room.

<hr/>

5

How long did I stay like that, lying as rigid as a corpse with my stifling quilt pulled up over my head? It seemed like an eternity, but it was probably only a few minutes. I didn't hear that muffled, irritatingly familiar sound again, but that didn't mean my nighttime visitor was gone. He . . . she . . . *it!* . . . could still be lurking out there, waiting for me. I alternated between fear of being strangled by the intruder and fear of suffocating from lack of air. Suffocation won out, and I decided I'd have to come up for a breath.

As slowly as possible, I edged my head out from under the heavy quilt. I lay as still as I could, gulping in the fresh air and straining to hear the slightest sound. The room was quiet as a tomb, and I decided my visitor must be gone. No one could be that quiet, except, of course, a ghost.

In a flash, the thought of a ghost had me right back under the quilt, burrowing into the mattress like a human mole. Even though it was at least a hundred degrees under there, I shivered and broke out in a cold sweat. Finally, though, that tiny, rational part of my brain spoke up, and I gave myself a fierce talking-to.

Kate (I began), some people at this lodge seem to believe in the possibility of a ghostly presence. But do you? Well (I answered) . . . maybe. And (I went on) even if it's not a ghost, then just who is it and what are they doing sneaking around here in the middle of the night?

Well, as you can imagine, this argument was so convincing that the rational part of my brain was completely cowed, and I was right back where I started, slowly suffocating under the quilt. At last, though, I couldn't stand it anymore, and I once again wormed my face out from under the covers. I worked up the courage to open my eyes. Slowly, I lifted my head and peered around.

At first, it seemed as if the room was filled with threatening shadowy figures, but one by one I identified all of them as the chintz rocking chair, the television, the wardrobe, the lamp. The place looked safe enough, unless, of course, someone was hiding in the bathroom.

I decided that risky as it might be, I had to make sure about that. As stealthily as I could, I slipped out of bed and crept over to the bathroom. Inside my chest, my heart was thumping wildly. I twisted the bathroom doorknob, closed my eyes, and yanked. Then I opened my eyes and screamed.

It took me a long moment to realize that the shadowy figure in front of me was my own reflection in the mirror on the door of the medicine cabinet. When the truth hit me, I laughed out loud in relief, not even caring if I sounded like mad Bertha.

Still smiling, I crossed the room and sank into the chintz rocker. I heard my mother's voice speaking inside my brain, nagging at me to be logical, to try to sort out my jumbled thoughts. I was in an unfamiliar place, and I'd heard a silly rumor about a ghostly legend. I was away from home by myself for the first time. I'd had a long, tiring bus ride and had had to meet a lot of odd strangers. I'd been disappointed about Monty's not showing up. I'd gorged myself on a rich, heavy meal. Plus I was anxious about going skiing the next day. Could I possibly have dreamed I'd heard a muffled sound in my room?

I decided I had. Or maybe I actually had heard a noise in the room, but it had undoubtedly been water in the pipes, or a creaky beam in the ceiling. My mother was always telling me I had an overactive imagination. For the first time in my life, I was actually happy to agree with her.

Completely reassured, I happily creaked back and forth in the comfortable, old rocker. Then, I remembered. The shock hit me like a bucket of ice water right in the face. I stopped rocking and gripped the arms of the chair, trying to convince myself it couldn't be true.

But it was true. The only thing in the seat of the chintz chair was my trembling body. There was no sign of the object I'd so carefully put there with my own two hands only a short time ago. Dad's precious leather suitcase had vanished into thin air.

———

6

Automatically, I started rocking again. Think, I told myself. You know for sure you put the suitcase on the chair. And it's not there now. So that proves that some kind of being, human or otherwise, was in the room. But how did that being get in?

Immediately, I conjured up an image of some slimy spirit oozing through the crack under the door. I realized my teeth were chattering like my dad's automatic hedge clippers. Get serious, Clancy! my inner voice shrieked. Try to make a token effort to act like an intelligent person. If you're determined to believe in this farfetched ghost theory, the least you can do is get out of this dumb rocking chair, check the windows and doors, and prove no human being could have stolen your suitcase. Then you can call in the ghostbusters!

On shivery, wobbly legs, I stood up and made myself totter to the window and look at the latch. So far, so bad. The window was tightly latched from the inside, and the spook-under-the-crack notion was still alive and well. But when I crossed the room to look at the door, I did a double take. At this point I was so prepared to accept the ghost notion, I was braced to find myself in front of a locked door. But I wasn't! Instead, the little brass safety chain was hanging straight down, loose from its hook.

All at once my legs refused to hold up my body anymore. With a sigh I sank down onto the floor. As my hands came into contact with the rag rug, I made another discovery. There were two small damp patches, side by side in front of the doorway. I crawled a little ways into the room until my fingers touched several more wet spots, and all at once I sat up and said, "Aha!"

Who would have thought I'd be relieved to discover that a person had broken into my room and stolen my suitcase? But relieved is just what I was, because now I was ninety-nine and forty-four one-hundredths percent sure that my creepy intruder hadn't been a ghost. After all, what kind of ghost has to open a safety chain to escape from a locked room, when all it would have to do is atomize through the wall? And, even more convincing, what kind of ghost leaves slightly snowy footprints on a rag rug?

The more I thought about it, the more I was sure I was right. Some way someone had gotten into my room, even with the window and door locked from the inside, just as Bobby's had been yesterday. But something had gone wrong. This "someone" had made a noise—a maddeningly familiar noise—that had woken me up and *House of Unspeakable Evil* had thumped onto the floor. The thump had scared the intruder, who had grabbed Dad's suitcase and run out the door before I could see him and find out who he was.

It all made sense except for one thing. None of it made any sense! Why in the world would anyone do something like that? Granted, Dad's suitcase was worth some money. But if the intruder was just a plain old thief, why hadn't he, or she, broken into my room when I was away at dinner instead of waiting till I was sound asleep in bed?

I had a nagging sense that the explanation for at least part of the puzzle was sneaking around somewhere inside my own mind, but I was so exhausted from fear and lack of sleep that I couldn't think straight. One part of me was advising me to leave the room and call for help, but another part said it would rather die than step out into the spooky hall in the middle of the night. Suddenly, my cozy bed seemed like the safest place to hide, at least until daylight.

With my last ounce of strength I pushed the chintz rocker up against the door and staggered back across the

41

room toward the bed. I lay quietly on the bed with my eyes half closed, teetering on the verge of sleep. A chorus line of vague, disturbed thoughts danced back and forth behind the curtains of my overworked consciousness. As I drifted off, one thought boogied out onto center stage and shook its fist at me, demanding to be noticed. Startled, I sat bolt upright. I jumped out of bed, ran over to the doorway, and snapped on the overhead light. I dropped to my knees and began crawling across the room, inspecting each inch of the rug and floorboards. Sherlock Holmes would have been jealous of my thoroughness.

Moments later I was back in bed, huddled in the quilt. "Of c-c-c-course," I said through my chattering teeth. "Of course." I'd just figured out part of the solution to the locked-room mystery—and now I was more scared than ever.

7

By six A.M. the next morning I was showered, dressed in yesterday's clothes, and out in the hall, ready to grope my way through the winding passageways to the lobby. I was locking my door when I heard a loud *boom* that sounded like a cannon going off. I gasped and huddled against the wall, sure that the lodge was being bombed. Several more booms followed, and then everything was quiet. I stood up straight again, surprised to see that the building was still standing.

As I shakily proceeded on my way, I realized what had happened. During his premovie lecture last night, Bobby had explained to me that many mountain lodges are in danger from avalanches, especially after heavy snows. Each morning the ski patrols go out and check the area. Sometimes they create mini avalanches in order to prevent big ones. They do this by shooting off a cannon, which was undoubtedly the source of the booms I'd heard.

When I entered the lobby, I saw jittery Camille, twitchy Lars, sniffly Pixie, and moody Peter standing just inside the front door. They were rubbing their hands and stamping snow off their boots, and I assumed they'd been out working on the avalanche problem.

The door opened and a short, stocky, frog-faced man blew in with a gust of cold air. "Six inches of new snow," he said in a croaky voice. He even sounded like a frog! "The powder freaks are going to go wild this morning." He pulled off his snowy cap and revealed that the top of his head was almost completely bald.

"I only hope they can get the road cleared in time for the traffic from the city, Ted," Camille said in a shrill voice. "I'd hate for the day skiers not to be able to get up here. Are you sure you made arrangements for the plows to do the entire road, instead of stopping at your place and leaving us stranded?"

"The crew is already well past my place, Camille," said the man. He gave her a sideways glance with his large, buggy eyes. "Not that you've been getting very many people coming up here lately. Not like the old days at Snowshoe. Why, I remember—"

"Kate!" Pixie's sharp voice carried across the lobby, and the older man stopped talking and stared at me. Suddenly, all of them were staring at me—and there wasn't a friendly-looking pair of eyeballs in the bunch.

"What are you doing up so early?" Pixie went on in a concerned voice. "Is something the matter?"

I came forward slowly. "Well," I began. "Someone—" I broke off, unsure what to do. It occurred to me that I didn't know whom I could trust around here. Some faceless stranger had sneaked into my room in the middle of the night and gone to great pains to make it look like he or she was a ghost. For all I knew, my creepy intruder had been one of the people standing right in front of me. Still, I had to trust someone. I took a deep breath and made up my mind. I'd start at the top of the chain of command, ditzy as it might be. "Camille," I said, "could I talk to you somewhere privately for a minute?"

The silence was broken only by the jingling of the charms on Camille's bracelet knocking against each other. "*Ah-choo!*" Pixie sneezed into a green tissue, and gave an apologetic laugh. "There's hot chocolate in the kitchen," she said. "Why don't you two get yourselves a couple of mugs full and go talk in Camille's office?"

Camille didn't move, and finally Pixie went through the dining room into the kitchen and came back out with two steaming mugs of hot chocolate. She handed me one cup and then practically threw the other one at the hotel owner. As the hot mug touched her hands, Camille blinked her eyes in surprise. Slowly, she moved in the direction of her office.

Inside the tiny, cluttered office, Camille cleared off a chair for me and sat down behind a large, messy desk. When she gazed at me, she looked so apprehensive, I wondered if she expected me to punch her in the nose.

"My suitcase vanished out of my room last night," I began.

I was ready to go on talking when, to my surprise and dismay, I saw Camille's tired brown eyes fill with tears. She put down her hot chocolate and started fiddling with her charms. I got a close look at them, and saw that they were tiny little golden skis. As Camille followed my gaze, she gave a bitter snort. "These charms are supposed to be good luck," she said. "My father gave them to me when I was a young girl first trying to succeed as a skier. Well, they may have been good luck once, but I have had nothing but bad luck lately. And now I am finished. I will have to close down."

"You're going to close down the hotel?" I repeated in amazement. "Because someone stole my suitcase?" It's not that I don't like being taken seriously, because I do. But even I, the Queen of the Dramatic Overreaction, thought Camille was being a tad extreme.

The dark-haired woman looked up at me with red,

discouraged eyes. "Oh, no," she said with a shuddering sigh. "It's not just your suitcase, though that must have been very frightening. But we have had many incidents this ski season that can only be described as unnatural. Some seem to be just playful pranks, like the ice water in your friend Bobby's boots. But others are more serious, like ski equipment disappearing when no one is there to take it, or the telephone lines mysteriously going dead. And—" I must have moved in my chair or something, because Camille seemed to suddenly remember I was there. Her uncontrolled flood of words evaporated as if a hot Santa Ana wind had just blown in from the desert. I wasn't surprised. I was amazed it had taken her this long to realize she was confiding all this stuff to a fourteen-year-old guest she'd met only the day before. She stared at me, and an embarrassed flush spread over her finely boned face.

I stared back at her and took a bracing swig of hot chocolate. Then I remembered what I'd really come to tell Camille. "Listen," I said, sitting forward on my chair, "last night, when my suitcase was stolen, the door and window were both locked, and—"

Camille interrupted me. "Another locked room," she gasped. "I have tried to tell myself it cannot be true. One of my staff came to me and said she had actually seen . . . something, and I argued with her. But how long can I continue to fly in the face of the evidence? These impossible things keep happening. And we have had so many things vanishing from locked rooms. The legend—can it be true?" Without even seeming to realize what she was doing, Camille reached out and picked up a pill bottle conveniently located on a corner of the desk.

"What exactly is the story about Snowshoe Lodge?" I asked her. "What is the old legend?"

A puzzled look came over the woman's face. "You know, it is strange," she said. "But I do not actually know what the Snowshoe Mountain legend is except that it is something to do with ghosts and unfriendly spirits. And something the Germans call a poltergeist. My late uncle Jacques was the one who built this lodge in the 1930's. He was quite an eccentric. He modeled this place after an old castle he once visited in Transylvania, and then decided to make it into a ski lodge!"

Camille laughed out loud, the pill bottle in her hand temporarily forgotten. I saw what she had probably been like before she'd become such a neurotic mess. As if she were reading my mind, she said, "I feel as if I haven't laughed in an eternity. But I used to laugh all the time before things began to go wrong around here. At first everything seemed to be going so well, but I made a few changes and . . ." Her voice trailed off, and the familiar worried, slightly dazed expression slowly reappeared on her face. I felt really sorry for her and realized that, in just the one day I'd known her, I'd come to like her quite a bit. That is, I liked her when she wasn't acting like a total space cadet, which she seemed to be on the verge of doing at this very moment as she slowly began twisting the pill bottle in her hands.

I decided to get her talking again. "You were telling

me about the legend of Snowshoe Mountain?" I prompted.

Camille looked bewildered. "That's the oddest thing," she said. "All my life I was told stories about cuckoo Uncle Jacques and his ski lodge in America. We heard he was strange, but we also heard the lodge was a thriving success, with some of the best skiing in the West. Yet none of us ever heard anything about a legend! In fact, I learned there was a ghostly legend only a few months ago. At first I scoffed. But now it seems I must believe in it because of all these mysterious happenings. Certainly everyone who comes to stay or work here soon becomes aware that unnatural things are going on here. And one person swears she *saw* . . . an unearthly phenomenon."

Even with an unidentified eyewitness, something about this legend stuff was starting to bother me. I wanted to ask Camille more about it, but I couldn't, because the office door opened and the bald-headed man from the lobby came in. Was there something familiar about his shape, or was it just that he reminded me of Kermit from *Sesame Street*?

"Excuse me, Camille," he said in his ribbity voice. "I know you're busy in here, but I wanted to let you know I'm on my way back down to Clementine's for breakfast."

"Of course, Ted," Camille answered absently. Her mind was obviously still thinking about what she'd been telling me.

The man bugged his round eyes at me, obviously wondering why I needed to talk to Camille privately at six A.M. "I hope you like powder skiing, young lady," he said heartily. "We've the best snow of the season, even down on the second-rate slopes at Sunburst!"

I started mumbling about how I'd never actually been skiing before on powder or anything else, when Camille returned to the present and remembered her manners. "Ted, this is Kate Clancy from Los Angeles," she said. "Kate, this is Mr. Tedley, the owner of Clementine's Hotel, down the road from us."

When froggy Mr. Tedley shook my hand, I was tempted to check for webs between his fingers. He chatted for a while longer in his hearty way, and then said goodbye and walked out of the office. As he left, I reflected that he had a serious inferiority complex about owning a lodge on Sunburst Mountain. But back to the business at hand. "Camille," I said in an urgent voice, "I don't know what's going on around here—or why. But I do think I've figured something out that might help you get rid of some of these mysterious stories you say have been floating around."

Camille put down her pill bottle, and her eyes sharpened with interest. She leaned forward in her chair to hear me. And I told her I had a theory about how the "ghost" had gotten in and out through my locked window and door.

8

Camille followed me back through the halls to my room.
On the way I told her about hearing the mysterious sound,
dropping my book, and finding the dangling safety chain
and wet footprints. When we were inside, I hit her with
the truly brilliant theory I'd worked out the night before.
"Since I knew the window had been latched, and I'd
fastened the safety chain after I came in," I said, "it struck
me that there was only one way someone could have been
in my room last night. And it's the same trick that was
played with Bobby's ski boots yesterday."

The lodge owner twisted her small hands and looked
anxiously around her, as if waiting for a spirit to materi-
alize over my shoulder. "You say you want to disprove the
ghost idea, Kate," she began anxiously. "But what you are
saying—"

"What I am saying," I broke in, "is that *someone was
already hiding in here* when I came in from dinner last
night!" Like a detective right out of one of my books, I
paced around the room. "They could have been in the
bathroom," I went on, "but I brushed my teeth in there,
so I know they weren't. They could have been under the
bed, but I looked under there, and only an undernourished
skeleton would have fit. So . . ." I paused to heighten the

effect of my speech. "They must have been hiding right in there the whole time!" With a dramatic wave of my arm, I flung open the doors to the old wooden wardrobe against the wall. I showed Camille where I'd found the soggy footprints on the rug. They'd evaporated by now, but last night they'd led from the door to the wardrobe.

The dark-haired woman looked so stunned that I wondered for a moment if she were putting on an act. "It is hard to believe," she said when she was able to speak, "that someone would go to such lengths just to steal a suitcase."

"The person must have been hiding in Bobby's wardrobe before he went into his room yesterday," I said, thinking out loud. "Then, during his shower, they slipped out, filled his boots with snow from the window ledge, and went back into hiding. Because the safety chain was still fastened, Bobby thought no one could have come in or out. But the person must have been right there in his room the whole time—waiting for a chance to sneak out after Bobby left!"

Instead of listening to my piercing logic, Camille was peering doubtfully into the dark, stuffy wardrobe. "This is a large armoire, to be sure, but it would not be very comfortable for an entire night, even for me. Obviously, the thief was able to get inside your room from the hall. So why did he not just take the suitcase and leave before you came in last night?" Camille never had gotten around to taking a pill back in her office, so her brain was clear enough to pose a pretty sharp question. She was finally beginning to resemble the efficient, competent lodge owner everyone had described at dinner last night.

But all at once I knew the answer to her question. "Because!" I cried triumphantly. "Because then everyone would have known he was just a regular thief who'd picked my lock in an ordinary thieflike way. But this way, with the chain fastened, we all believed only a ghost could have done it. You said you'd been having mysterious disappearances from locked rooms all ski season—well, this is the explanation! Someone is impersonating a ghost around here! Someone wants people to believe that Snowshoe Mountain Lodge is haunted!"

"But why?" Camille asked. "Why would anyone want that?"

Well, she had me stumped. I mean, I guess I can only figure out one "why" at a time. I'd been so smug about working out the mystery of the locked room, I hadn't made much progress on working out the thief's grand plan. That is, if he had a grand plan and wasn't just a plain old crackpot.

And speaking of crackpots, Camille was looking more sane by the minute, as if the idea of tracking down a human criminal appealed to her a lot more than having a priest exorcise the spooks from the lodge. She thought for a while, and said she'd have Peter check the locks on all the rooms and see if he couldn't figure out some way of making them more secure, so the phony ghost couldn't keep getting into the rooms. Then she looked at her watch and said she had to go supervise breakfast.

As she hurried away, it occurred to me that she'd never once mentioned the idea of calling in the police to help find my suitcase. It seemed like the obvious thing to do, especially now that we were sure (well, almost sure) that we were dealing with a flesh-and-blood thief. It struck me as odd that Camille hadn't thought of it, but what else is new? Everything about this looney-bird lodge struck me as odd.

What I was thinking about now was breakfast. Remember, I'd been up most of the night with my teeth chattering and my heart racing in fifth gear. I felt like I'd just run a psychological Boston Marathon, and I was starving. After one more half-scared, half-mad look at the wardrobe, I decided to abandon the scene of the crime and go out and forage for food.

I'd gone back and forth between my room and the lobby so many times by now that I thought I knew the way by heart, and I became overconfident. Thus, I took a few wrong turns, and by the time I got to the dining room, most of the tables were at least partly full. I found the nearest empty chair and sat down.

The kids at my table all went to Valley High in Sherman Oaks together and acted as if they were lifelong friends. The only two I recognized were the boys who'd sat across the aisle from me on the bus. When I sat down, they stared at me like I was E.T.'s sister. Then they went back to guffawing about some stupid food fight they'd had in their school cafeteria.

I ordered pancakes and ate as quickly as I could, pondering the events of last night and trying not to listen to the inane conversation at the table. These kids didn't seem to be thinking about ghosts or thieves, or anything besides stuffing their Neanderthal faces. Soon, though, they started talking about how the ski school worked, and I perked up my ears. Apparently Darwin, one of the boys from the bus, had skied at Snowshoe last winter. He said that on the first morning of the week—today—all the skiers would gather at the top of Powderpuff Slope. While the ski instructors and everyone else watched, each person would have to ski down the hills. Based on this performance, Darwin explained, we would all be assigned to the correct classes. He was positive that he'd be put in the expert group this year.

I was so horrified, I stopped eating. "You can't mean it!" I burst out. "How can I ski down the hill in front of everybody? I've never even been on skis before!"

For a minute I thought no one was going to bother to lower himself to speak. Darwin finally took pity on me. "If you're a rank beginner," he explained, "you just go and stand at the bottom of the hill. The instructor will find you there."

It was obvious they all found me ignorant beyond belief. I ate the rest of my breakfast in total silence, chewing quietly as Darwin continued to talk about the ski school. Now he was giving his evaluation of each of the instructors. The other kids were listening to him like he was the Swami of Snowshoe.

"Peter Shade is pretty good," he said generously. "I heard he wants to be a racer, even though his mom says she doesn't want him to. Last year he tried to run away and turn pro, but his mom made him come back." He crunched some bacon, and the lecture continued. "Camille's okay, though she's not exactly a world-class skier. Pixie's a fairly swift skier, but she can have a real temper if you don't do what she tells you. Last year some people tried to drop out of her classes because of it. But I hope I get Lars Lundquist. He was a racer in Sweden, you know, before he went nuts or something, and he and I could probably give each other some pointers. Last year Camille had him teaching the beginners. What a waste!"

What a jerk! I thought. I was so eager to get away from that conceited twerp, I actually left a few bites of breakfast on my plate! As I hurried out of the dining hall, I collided with the large mass of Bobby Berman and once again was surprised at how glad I was to see his chubby face. In some ways Bobby was starting to remind me of Puffbear, the stuffed animal I still occasionally turn to in times of crisis. The two of them really have quite a lot in common. They're both big, round, and reassuring somehow. The main difference is that Bobby still has both of his ears and isn't covered with matted blue fur.

Anyway, true to his word, Bobby took me to the rental shop in the basement and helped me get fitted for skis, poles, and boots. On the way I wondered if I should tell him about my not-so-ghostly visitor of last night. But Bobby was babbling on so enthusiastically about the great skiing conditions, etc., etc., I didn't have the heart—or the volume—to bring up such an unpleasant subject.

While Bobby was carrying my equipment outside for me, I ran back to my room for my jacket, mittens, and hat. When I got to my hall, I had a real shock. A man was down on his knees in front of my door peering through my lock! I must have made some kind of noise, because the man turned around and stared at me. Then I saw it was Peter Shade.

He gave me his slightly satanic but devastating smile. Be still, my foolish heart! "Hello, there, Kate," he said. "Camille asked me to take a look at your lock."

I wondered how much he knew about what had happened last night. But I didn't say anything, because as usual with Peter, I couldn't think of anything to say. He got to his feet. "I'll see what I can do this afternoon," he said. "Though I'm afraid these old locks are pretty easy to pick. I might have to put in dead bolts."

Dead bolts, I thought. The terminology couldn't have been more appropriate for this morgue of a place. I glanced at Peter and saw that he was frowning, which caused his thick, dark eyebrow to form an angry V over his eyes. "I'm not going to be able to make *any* repairs," he said, "if I can't find my tool belt. It seems to have disappeared from the hook in the lobby overnight."

With that parting remark, Peter left, and I went into

my room, where I studiously avoided looking at the wooden wardrobe. I found my new purple mittens and hat in my jacket pocket, but realized my matching purple-and-white scarf must have been packed inside my unfortunate suitcase. Oh, well, I told myself. It was warm and sunny outside anyway. I stuffed some money for my lift ticket into my pocket and hurried back out into the hall.

Before long I was staggering around outside in the soft snow, trying to stand up in my bulky ski boots. Fortunately, Bobby saw me and told me to put my heel down before my toe when I took a step. That really helped, even if it didn't exactly transform me into a ballerina. We walked over to where Bobby had left our skis, stuck like Excalibur in a snowbank.

He was very patient about helping me, although he did make so many loud suggestions that at least fifty people stopped to stare. Even with his assistance it took forever to get my skis on. I was supposed to put my toe into the front of the binding on the ski and stamp down hard with my heel, causing the binding to snap shut. The first few times I tried, it didn't work because I had globs of snow stuck on the bottom of my boot. When Bobby tried to clean it off, I had to balance on one foot. Naturally I ended up toppling over right on top of him. After we succeeded in getting one ski on, we had to go through the exact same thing with the other one!

When I was finally ready to go, Bobby snapped on his

skis in about two seconds. "We have to go buy our lift tickets," he boomed, reaching out for my crumpled bills. "Follow me."

I tried to imitate Bobby's long, sweeping stride and immediately crossed the tips of my skis and fell over. I'd probably still be flopping around out there if Pixie hadn't come along and given me a hand up. She gave me a sympathetic, sniffly smile. "Don't worry, Kate," she said. "You'll get the hang of it." Pixie had been so nice to me, I decided not to believe what Darwin had said about her temper at breakfast. It occurred to me that Darwin himself had probably been one of the people who'd tried to drop out of her class last winter. Good riddance, I thought, as I struggled on my way.

By the time I reached the ticket window, I was ready to call it a day. If I couldn't even *walk* on skis, how was I ever going to *ski* on them? The only way I could make any progress at all was to take teensy little shuffling steps forward at the rate of about six inches a minute.

Bobby got my lift ticket for me and showed me how to put it on. He looped a slender, curved wire through the hole in my zipper tab and then folded the sticky ticket over the square end of the wire. "Whatever you do, Clance," he said, "don't lose your ticket. You can't get on the chair lift without it."

Powderpuff Slope was just to the left of the ticket office. Even to my terrified eyes it looked reassuringly short and flat. Most of skiers were riding something called a J-bar lift up to the top of the slope. Soon I spotted a few straggly, anxious-looking people standing at the bottom of the hill and figured they had to be the other beginners. With my short, shuffling steps, I inched my way toward them.

The tryouts had already begun, and we all craned our necks to see. Pixie, Camille, and Lars were standing at the bottom of the hill. As each skier came down toward them, they discussed which class to put the person in. As far as I could tell, Pixie seemed to be making most of the decisions about who should go where, though every now and then Lars would make a comment and Camille would listen intently and nod, while Pixie shrugged or stared off into space. Usually, though, the three of them seemed to agree pretty quickly.

Just then I saw the knowledgeable Darwin from breakfast appear at the top. He pointed himself straight down the hill and took off at top speed, making almost no turns as he went. When he reached the bottom, he skidded to a stop in a huge spray of snow. Pixie started to point him in one direction, but Camille and Lars spoke briefly and waved him over to where Peter, looking somewhat bored and aloof, was standing with a small group of people. Someone nearby said that was the advanced intermediate class. Darwin didn't look very happy, but I was overjoyed.

After that I saw Bobby appear at the top of the slope. He started down, making a series of tight, precise little turns. Even my ignorant eyes could tell that Bobby was a fantastic skier. He looked elegant and in complete control somehow. And amazingly enough, he didn't even look that chubby up there. Pixie told him to stand next to her. I knew she was the teacher for the experts.

Now only one person remained at the top of the hill. There was no mistaking Lynda Dalton's blond hair and vivid red jumpsuit. Even from this distance, I was sure I saw her gaze wistfully down at Peter's class.

At last Lynda moved forward and immediately fell down hard. She shook her hair and got to her feet. And fell again. She struggled up and began fiddling with the buckle on her ski boot. After a long time she started moving slowly across the hill. She picked up some speed and suddenly sat down with a bang. This time she didn't get up but kept sliding along on her bottom. Finally, about halfway down, she came to a dead stop.

I was thunderstruck. This was the person who'd told Peter that skiing was an essential part of the core of her being? Two minutes later Camille was leading her to the bottom of the hill. I thought I heard Lynda muttering something about the poor conditions on Powerpuff Slope. But I didn't really listen. I was too busy trying not to laugh. Lynda Dalton had been put in the same class with me and the other *rank* beginners.

9

Lars turned out to be the teacher for the beginners again this year, so I guessed poor Darwin would have to be deprived of the chance to exchange ideas on racing technique with him. There were only five of us in the class: me; Lynda; a short, freckle-faced girl named Annie, whom I vaguely knew from algebra class at Pacifico; Ralph Nickerson, a white-haired retired insurance agent from Phoenix; and Nita Nickerson, his short little wife.

We spent the first hour or so learning how to walk forward, sideways, and uphill on skis. More importantly, we learned how to get up once we'd fallen down. It was all pretty boring, but there was no denying I desperately needed the instruction. But bad as I was, I was nowhere near as awful as Ralph from Phoenix. In fact, he was so awkward, it almost looked like he was deliberately tripping himself up. He seemed like such a nice guy that I wondered if he could be putting on a clumsy performance to make the rest of us feel better about our own three left feet.

Anyway, Lars turned out to be a wonderful instructor. At first I'd had my doubts. After all, Darwin had said Lars used to be a racer (and hadn't he also said something about Lars going nuts? I wished now I'd listened more carefully . . .), and I couldn't figure out what a racer would have to say to a bunch of klutzes like us. But in fact he seemed to understand just what we were going through and to be able to pinpoint what we were doing wrong. And amazing as it seemed, he actually appeared to be enjoying himself! I checked out his eyes a couple of times, but there was no sign of his nervous twitch.

Soon Lars told us he thought we were ready for the thrill of going up the hill. He showed us how to stand in the ski tracks, put the J-bar behind our rear ends, and hold on for dear life while we were towed upward. I had the bad luck to be the first one to try it, and with my usual dexterity I immediately fell down and couldn't get back up again.

When I finally did reach the top, I looked back and saw that everyone else was having the same problems I'd had; dropping the bar, skidding out of the tracks, and falling down. Ralph actually managed to get the tip of his long ski cap tangled up in the lift somehow, causing the whole mechanism to shut down.

During the next hour Lars taught us how to ski across the hill at a snail's pace, with the tips of our skis close together and the backs stuck way out sideways. At the end of each trip we were supposed to make what he called a wedge turn, which involved slowly shifting our weight to the outside ski and coming around in a small circle. I must have fallen down about fifty times, but so did everyone else in the class. After a while we were all following Ralph's example and getting into the spirit of helping each other out. When one of us had to ski down the slope alone, the rest of us would stand to one side and shout words of encouragement. By the end of the morning we were all making silly wisecracks and slapping each other on the back, feeling like we were the best of friends.

Lynda was the only one who didn't have a good time. She spent most of the lesson in a major-league sulk. When it was her turn to ski, she would go a few feet and then fall down and refuse to get up. Lars was very patient with her, pretending not to notice she was acting like a complete cretin.

Lynda's response to all this patience was to arrange her Kewpie-doll mouth into a perfect pout. By lunchtime I was ready to sock her right in the lip gloss. But fortunately the lesson came to an end before I was driven to violence in the snow.

We all took off our skis and trooped into the lodge, where I saw Lars opening a large locker in the front of the lobby. "I don't eat lunch," he explained, "but I keep my carrot juice in here. It saves me the trip back to my condo behind the hotel. I always choose Locker 13, so I'll remember which one I'm using." As I watched, he pulled out a jar of the most nauseating, oozy, orange liquid I'd ever seen in my life. Behind the jar there was a lot of other junk in the locker, like extra mittens and socks, some kind of toolbox, and a pair of shoes. It looked like Lars regarded old Locker 13 as a real home away from home.

I thanked Lars for the lesson and went to join Annie, Ralph, and Nita. We hung our jackets on hooks in the lobby and stomped into lunch together. Soon I heard Bobby's booming voice behind me and turned to see him coming in with Pixie and two other expert skiers. I was sure he'd come over to our table, and in spite of my new affection for him, I cringed at having to introduce Ralph and Nita to my loudmouthed friend. Instead, though, he gave me a wave and sat down in the corner with the rest of his class. Don't ask me why, but that didn't make me happy either.

Just then Peter Shade came in, and all thoughts of Mouth Berman left my bedazzled brain. Peter's long face was darkly tanned from the sun, which made his black eyes look even more mysterious and intriguing. His normally smooth hair was falling dramatically across his forehead with its V-shaped frowning eyebrow. For one glorious moment I thought he was heading toward me, but then Lynda materialized behind him and spoke into his ear. He turned and followed her to an empty table in the far corner. I sighed and decided to concentrate on what Ralph and Nita were saying.

Well, as it turned out, Nita wasn't saying much of anything. Ralph, on the other hand, was holding forth (at length) on some of the more fascinating aspects of selling insurance. I wondered why he thought anyone outside the world of insurance would possibly be interested in so many boring details about his job.

My nose started quivering, and I saw that the waiters and waitresses were carrying in big tureens of thick vegetable soup along with platters of fresh-baked bread, as well as cheese and meat. Camille herself served our table. She was looking less zombielike all the time, a fact that

I took complete credit for, since it was my ghost-busting discovery that had helped buck up her spirits this morning. She had a long, friendly chat with Ralph and Nita, during which it was revealed that they'd been staying at Snowshoe since early December. It was hard to believe they'd been here for over two months and were still such awful skiers!

As she was about to leave, Camille turned to me. "I can see you are someone who appreciates good food, Kate," she said. (I was already halfway through my second bowl of soup.) "Tonight I think you will be pleased. I am preparing my famous chocolate mousse torte."

I couldn't say anything because my mouth was full of hot soup, but I tried to put on an enthusiastic expression. To me, chocolate mousse is one of the things that make life worth living.

When Camille was gone, Ralph lowered his voice and started talking about how tired the hotel owner looked. "I guess it's no secret she's been having problems around the inn," he said. "What with all this strange legend business. I wonder if anything else has happened." With surprisingly penetrating gray eyes, he looked around the table expectantly, as if hoping one of us would come up with a story as juicy as the jar in Lars's locker.

And of course I had a juicy story. But I wasn't about to tell just anyone about my suitcase. I mean, Camille hadn't exactly pledged me to secrecy, but now that we knew the thief was most likely human, how did I know whom I could trust? Why, I didn't even completely trust Camille herself! And the more time I spent with Ralph, the louder my phoniness detector crackled.

Anyway, I was saved from having to say anything, because just then Lars came by our table to say hello. "I'm glad to see you are all together," he said with his movie-star smile. "I wanted to tell you that in the afternoons we have free skiing, with no classes. But tomorrow morning we will meet again at the bottom of Powderpuff and conquer the mountain."

We all smiled at this ridiculous idea, and Nita invited Lars to eat with us, but he said he'd already had his carrot juice and had to rush off to give a private lesson. After Lars left, Ralph suddenly announced that he wasn't hungry, and said he and Nita were going back out to the hill to practice. I watched them follow Lars out of the dining room and saw Peter, Lynda, and Pixie walk out right after them.

This semi-mass exodus made me feel a little guilty. But Annie and I agreed we were in no hurry to leave the warm dining room and begin brutalizing our bodies again. We sat back in our chairs, ordered more hot chocolate, and gossiped about some kids we knew from Pacifico.

Three and a half cups later we were finally ready to return to the Great Outdoors. We waddled back out to the lobby to retrieve our jackets and caps. As Annie zipped herself into her electric-blue parka, I found myself staring at her. Something about her jacket had changed since that morning. But what?

She pointed at me and said, "Hey, Kate, what happened to your lift ticket?"

I quickly touched the end of my zipper. But instead of the familiar sticky paper, there was only a jagged piece of broken wire. I realized then what was different about Annie's jacket as well. The dangling green-and-white rectangle was missing. While we'd been in the dining room eating lunch, someone had come along and stolen our lift tickets.

10

Tears ran down Annie's freckled cheeks. "Gosh, Kate," she said. "I don't have enough money to pay for another lift ticket. My dad figured out just how much I was going to need for this trip, and he didn't give me a single extra penny."

I had the exact same problem, but I told Annie not to worry, even though I was worrying like a maniac myself. As I patted her arm, I looked around at the other jackets in the lobby and saw that a lot of them were missing their lift tickets. The thief must have raced through and grabbed as many tickets as possible. It seemed like a risky thing to do with people coming in and out of the dining room, but obviously he or she had timed it perfectly.

Just then Peter Shade and his mother, Marsha, came out of the office into the lobby. Peter started to give me his scintillating, inscrutable smile but noticed something was wrong. He and his mother hurried over to Annie and me. I held up my piece of jagged wire. "Someone stole our lift tickets," I said. "And lots of others, too." To my dismay, my voice sounded all quavery, as if I were ready to cry.

Marsha Shade drew in her breath sharply. "This is really going too far, Peter!" she said in a low, angry voice.

"I agree," said Peter. "It's going to be hard to blame the ghost for this one." His voice didn't sound angry, but more flat, dead, and discouraged. He didn't look at his mother, and she didn't look at him, but I sensed they were really talking to each other anyway.

Suddenly Marsha went into action. She wheeled around and went back into the office. Seconds later she returned with a stack of wires and lift tickets. With an abrupt motion she thrust half of them at Peter. "Hurry!" she snapped. "Replace all the missing tickets you can find. Maybe we can cover this up . . . *again.*" The last word was muttered in such a low voice, I almost didn't hear it.

But Peter obviously did. As he took the pile of lift tickets from his mother, his face darkened. "Who do you think you're fooling . . . ?" he began.

But Marsha wasn't listening. She was on her knees, swiftly putting new tickets on Annie's jacket and mine. With a frustrated sigh, Peter turned away and got to work

68

replacing the tickets on the rest of the jackets in the lobby.

Annie didn't have a clue about what was going on, and I only had the clear certainty that my midnight visitor, whom I was coming to think of as the Snowshoe Prankster, had struck again. What I couldn't figure out were the ominous undercurrents between Peter and Marsha Shade. Neither one of them had seemed particularly surprised by the theft of the lift tickets. And each one of them had acted as if the other one had some sort of guilty knowledge! Once again no one had mentioned calling in the police to investigate the robbery (which, with each lift ticket costing twenty dollars, was no small potatoes moneywise). The notion of a cover-up came back into my mind.

As Annie and I stood around like a couple of awkward galumphs, Peter and his mother frantically replaced stolen lift tickets. So far luck was with them, and no one had caught them at it. But at that very moment Bobby Berman clomped out of the dining room and took his jacket off its hook.

A quick glance told me that Bobby's ticket was gone, and that Peter and Marsha hadn't had a chance to give him a new one. Unlike Annie and me, he noticed his missing ticket right away. "Hey!" he hollered. "What the heck's going on here?" He'd increased his usual loud volume by about two full twists of the knob.

Peter and Marsha whirled around and stared at him in horror. Then Marsha ran up to Bobby, grabbed his large arm, and dragged him across the lobby into the front parlor. Without really knowing what I was doing, I followed them.

"Give me your jacket," Marsha told Bobby in a low, urgent voice. "I'll give you a new lift ticket."

"But what happened to the old one?" Bobby asked. His voice was at its usual earsplitting decibel level, and Marsha's tired black eyes became alarmed. "Be quiet, you fool!" she ordered.

Well, Bobby may have a thick hide, but even he began to notice he wasn't exactly being treated like Charles and Diana on a royal visit. A truculent look came over his round face, and Marsha suddenly realized she'd gone too far. She forced herself to smile. The effect in her tired, anxious face was ghastly. "I'm sorry," she said. "Some . . . er . . . child . . . has been playing a few pranks around the lodge, and I seem to have lost my sense of humor about it. We . . . my son and I . . . are trying to rectify what happened before too many guests are inconvenienced."

Bobby's face cleared, and he nodded politely and let Marsha fasten a new ticket onto his jacket. With another fake-o smile, the bookkeeper hurried out of the room to the lobby. Bobby and I stayed behind in the parlor. He was unnaturally quiet. Then he looked down at the remnants of his old ticket. "Gosh," he said profoundly. "Someone must have come through the lobby with a pair of wire cutters and started snipping like a maniac. These wires are really strong; the only way to get an old one off is to peel off the old ticket, and that takes forever."

Fleeting thoughts of tool belts and boxes drifted in and out of my head. Bobby wandered over to the large French windows that overlooked one of the ski slopes. All at once he whirled around to face me. "Clancy," he announced, "strange and mysterious forces are at work around here."

No kidding, I replied, but not out loud. Actually, I was relieved to have the subject out in the open. I'd been longing to confide in someone, and I decided it might as well be Bobby, particularly now that I'd noticed his resemblance to Puffbear. I made him sit down in one of the big old couches in front of the French windows. I told him everything I knew, including the shadowy figure outside our windows, his own snow-in-the-boots episode, and my midnight intruder and suitcase thief. When I told him my theory about the prankster's hiding in the wardrobes in the locked rooms, his eyes almost bugged out of his rotund head.

"But wait a minute," he said. "If the ghost . . . er, person . . . was going to hide in my wardrobe, why'd he need to be lurking around in the shadows outside my room?"

"How should I know?" I answered irritably. I'd been hoping he'd congratulate me on my brilliant detective work, but instead he'd immediately noticed an inconsistency I'd completely overlooked. "Maybe there's more than one person involved."

"Hmmm," Bobby said. "Hmmmm." He hoisted himself up out of the creaky old couch and went over to the

French windows again. Once again, he whirled around and faced me. "Motive!" he whispered dramatically. "Why, why, why?"

Well, Bobby's whisper is about the same volume as a normal person's shriek of terror, so when he spoke, I almost jumped out of my skin. As I slowly recovered from the shock, I began to think about what he'd said.

"Motive," I repeated slowly. "*Why* did someone steal all those lift tickets in the lobby?"

"Well, for one thing, you can usually resell a lift ticket at the hill," Bobby said. "People come up and want to ski for a few hours in the afternoon but don't want to pay for a whole day's ticket, so they buy a stolen one instead."

"Ah," I said. "The old financial-gain story. But some-how . . . I think there's more involved here than that." I glanced nervously over my shoulder at the door to the lobby. "But we can't talk here, Bobby. Somebody will walk in on us."

Bobby rubbed his chins. "You're right, Clance," he said. Was it my imagination, or was he talking out of the side of his mouth, like Humphrey Bogart? "Meet me for hot chocolate before dinner later. The dining room would probably still be empty around five-thirty."

He headed toward the door. "In the meantime, Clance," he said over his shoulder, "keep your eyes and ears open. The smallest thing might turn out to be a clue that could crack this caper wide open."

Yes, I hadn't imagined it. He was definitely talking out of one side of his mouth. All he needed was a trench coat and floppy hat. I followed him out to the lobby and looked for Annie, but there was no sign of her. She was probably already back on the slopes, practicing her wedge turns. Suddenly I was actually eager to get outside and indulge in some grueling physical activity that would force all this disturbing mystery stuff right out of my mind. I decided to run to my room to use the bathroom and put more sun block on my nose. Then I'd go back out, find Annie at the hill, and concentrate on keeping my weight on my downhill ski.

I got back to Room 13 in record time. The door was only open a crack, but it was enough to let me hear the sound. Footsteps coming from the inside. On cue, my heart went into its familiar jump-and-thump routine. There was no mistake about it. Once again, someone was walking around in my room.

11

I know I should have turned right around and run back to the lobby for help. But for a split second I was too scared to move. And while I stood rooted like a tree Johnny Appleseed had planted in the doorway, someone grabbed my arm and pulled me into the room. I closed my eyes in fear. Before I knew it, two strong arms were holding me tight.

I came to my senses and started to fight back. My arms were pinned to my sides, but my legs were free. With my eyes still shut, I brought my knee up into my captor's stomach.

"Oooofff!" The strong arms released me, and I heard a body slump to the floor. I found the courage to open my eyes. My cousin Monty was lying at my feet, clutching her middle.

"Oops." I got down on my knees. "Are you all right?"

Monty sat up and glared at me. "I was just trying to give you a hug," she said. "If you didn't want one, all you had to do was *tell* me!"

"Oh, Monty, I'm sorry!" I reached over and hugged her as hard as I could. "I'm so glad to see you. What are you doing here anyway? I thought you were sick."

"I convinced my dad I was better. It was only a dumb cold in the first place. I couldn't believe he was going to try to keep me home because of it."

I could believe it. Uncle Clark, Monty's father, is my mother's brother. I looked at my cousin and saw that her nose was a little red around the edges. But she still looked great. My mom's always trying to tell me that Monty and I look a lot alike, but I've never really believed it. It's true we have the same gray eyes and fuzzy hair, but somehow on Monty they're dramatic and arty, while on me they're just gray and fuzzy.

Monty got up, sat down on the chintz chair, and began pulling off her red cowboy boots. "Anyway, I got here as soon as I could," she said. "I thought you'd be pleased, but instead you engage me in hand-to-hand combat!"

I perched on the edge of the bed. "I thought you were something . . . er, *someone* else," I began, glancing nervously over at our wooden wardrobe. "It's the most unbelievable story. . . ."

"You'll have to tell me later," Monty said, in her usual dictatorial style. She reached for her battered black ski boots and began expertly buckling them on. "I missed the tryouts for the ski-school classes this morning, so the acting head of the ski school . . . the short one with the cold—"

"Pixie."

"Right. Pixie wants me to come out and ski for her now so she can assign me to a class for tomorrow morning. By the way, is it really true loopy Lars Lundquist from Sweden is an instructor here now?"

"Yes it is. In fact, he's my instructor! But how come you called him *loopy* Lars Lundquist?"

"It's a long story," Monty said. "It'll have to wait till after my ski tryout. Are you coming along?"

"Okay," I said. "I'll cheer you on." We locked our room and walked through the lobby and out the door. Outside, Monty had her skis snapped on before I'd even figured out which one of mine went on which foot.

"Hurry up, Kate," Monty said. "I'm going to be late."

I felt a quick rush of irritation, which I tried to ignore. As I mentioned earlier, Monty likes calling the shots with people. And she's so athletic, she tends to be impatient with normal mortals like me. But I was determined not to let my too-perfect cousin start bugging me this early in our visit. I forced a phony smile, à la Marsha Shade. "Why don't you go on over to Powderpuff and meet Pixie? I'll see you there."

When Monty was gone, I decided to carry my skis to the hill and put them on there. I'd noticed other people carrying both of theirs with the bottoms together, sticking them up over one shoulder like a soldier with a gun. I tried this for a while, but for some reason my skis wouldn't stay together like everyone else's, and I kept dropping one of them. I turned sideways with my burden and almost cracked open the head of another skier who was walking by.

At last I took one ski and one pole in each hand and marched the rest of the way to the hill. The stuff was pretty heavy, and my fingers started to ache, but fortunately Powderpuff wasn't very far away.

By the time I got there, Monty was already at the top of the slope and Pixie was waiting at the bottom. Lars was standing a few yards away. Nearby I saw Peter, fiddling with his skis. Just then I heard Bobby's unmistakable tones, and I turned to see him skiing in my direction. Annie was scuttling along behind him, battling valiantly to keep up.

"Hi, Kate," Annie gasped when they'd reached my side. "Bobby says he'll ski with us this afternoon and give us some pointers."

"Who is that?" Instantly, Bobby's foghorn voice had every head within a ten-mile area looking our way. Then they all turned their glances upward, to see whom he was asking about.

Of course, it was Monty. She was floating down the slope like a bird, taking a ride on a current of air in the sky. Unlike everyone else who'd stayed on the flat, packed snow in the center of the hill, she was skiing through some thick powder over by the woods at the trail's edge. As she snaked through the heavy stuff, she sent little arcs of puffy snow behind her.

"Who is that?" Bobby asked again.

Here we go again, I said to myself. "That's my cousin," I said shortly. "She just got here from Denver."

When Monty reached the bottom of the hill, she stopped to talk to Pixie. I was sure she'd be assigned to the expert class Bobby was in. A minute later she skated over to my side.

She looked down at my feet. "You still don't have your skis on?" she asked. "Are you planning to go sledding this afternoon?"

Before I could come up with a sarcastic retort, Peter Shade skied up and slid to a stop. He was as dangerously handsome as ever, but for once he looked interested and enthusiastic instead of angry and brooding. Lynda was nowhere around. She'd probably run back inside to search for a shade of eye shadow that would show up through her goggles.

"Hi, Kate," Peter said. He turned to Monty. "I understand you're Kate's cousin. We're glad you finally made it."

I introduced them and began fumbling around with my right ski, trying to get it lined up so I could step onto it without falling over sideways.

Peter cleared his throat. "Uh . . . I was wondering, Monty," he said, "if you'd like to ski together for a while this afternoon. I've been trying to find someone willing to go down Suicide Run with me, and I thought you might be interested."

Well, that figured. Boys always lost their hearts to Monty. I told myself I didn't mind that much. If I couldn't have Peter, which I'd never fooled myself for a minute I could, I'd much rather he like Monty than yucky Lynda. I stomped down hard on my ski, but of course the binding didn't click. I began gouging at the snow on the bottom of my boot, waiting to hear Monty say she'd love to ski Suicide Run with Peter.

But she didn't. "That's sounds like fun, Peter," she said. "But I really came to Snowshoe to ski with Cousin Kate here. That is, if she can ever manage to get her skis on. Maybe we can try Suicide later in the week."

I knew my cousin would kill me if I threw my arms around her right in front of everybody, but I almost did it anyway. Of course, it all made sense. Monty might be bossy and impatient and too perfect sometimes (all the time), but she was the same person she'd always been. I should have known she wouldn't dump me for some strange boy within a few minutes of arriving. She wouldn't be Monty if she acted like that. And she wouldn't be my best friend, either.

12

Bobby and Monty took turns giving Annie and me skiing lessons. Monty was okay, but Bobby turned out to be an amazingly good instructor. First he told us to follow along behind him and turn exactly when he turned. Usually I couldn't keep up and fell down almost immediately, but once or twice I really sensed myself getting into the rhythm of his effortless swings back and forth across the hill. At other times Bobby stood at the bottom of the trail and watched us ski toward him. As we came down, he would shout surprisingly helpful suggestions at us, and of course we had no trouble hearing him. (For that matter, neither did the people at the top of the mountain!)

By about three o'clock, Annie and I were worn out. Bobby and Monty went off to ski some harder trails, and Annie and I went inside. About an hour and a half later, Monty met me back in Room 13. She was raving about Snowshoe Mountain. "This is a fantastic ski area," she said, throwing herself onto her bed. "We met that great-looking boy Peter up at the top, and we all went down

Suicide Run together. It was really hard, but terrific! We're going to do it again tomorrow afternoon. He told me all about how he wants to turn pro as soon as he gets out of high school."

She pulled off her ski boots and started rubbing her toes through her red socks. "Now," she ordered, "please tell me this mysterious story of yours. I'm dying to hear it." As she spoke, she reached into her suitcase, which lay on the floor by her bed. She clawed around for a minute. Then her long fingers came out, clutching two bags of peanut M&M's. I was impressed. A treasure like that would never have lasted so long in my possession.

Blissfully sucking the thin candy shell off my first peanut, I sprawled on my own bed and spilled the beans about everything, just as I had to Bobby in the front parlor a few hours before. I described all the people I'd met here, along with all their unbelievable quirks. As I talked, I warmed to my subject and really built up the drama and suspense of my tale, starting with Bobby's friends and their story about a spooky legend, and working up to my hearing that maddeningly familiar sound in the dead of night. By the time I got to my vanishing suitcase, my cousin's gray eyes were popping out of her head.

In fact, my saga was going over so well, I almost hated to tell her I was now convinced the intruder had been human; but I didn't want to leave anything out, so I described finding the wet footprints leading to the big wardrobe. Before the words were out of my mouth, Monty jumped to her feet, ran over to the wardrobe, and pulled open the doors. She hunched her long, thin body into a ball and climbed inside. "I suppose it's *possible*," she said with her chin on her chest, "but why in the world would someone do such a crazy thing?"

I popped another M&M's and got to my feet. "That's the very question I've been wondering about all day," I said. "Motive. Why in the world would someone do all these crazy things? And after a lot of thought, I've concluded—"

"Loopy Lars!" Monty broke in rudely. Annoyed at being interrupted in mid monologue, I turned to glare at my cousin. Unfortunately, she was still curled up inside the wardrobe and didn't even see my expression.

"What about Loopy Lars?"

"You asked me why he was known as loopy," she reminded me. She stuck one of her long legs out of the wardrobe and grunted with pain. "And you started talking about crazy things. I don't see how any normal human being could have stayed in this place for five minutes! I vote for a midget ghost! Oof!" She half climbed, half fell out of the wardrobe.

I walked over and looked down at her. "All right, tell me. Why is Lars Lundquist known as Loopy Lars?"

"I'm surprised you don't know," Monty said, getting to her feet. "It was in all the ski magazines."

"My taste in reading is more literary than yours," I said loftily. "Just get on with the story."

"All right, all right. It happened about two years ago or so. Lars Lundquist was the up-and-coming hotshot on the Swedish racing team, their big hope for all the prizes on the racing circuit and maybe even a medal at the Olympics. And then, right before his first big downhill race, he snapped his twig."

"Snapped his twig?"

"Right. He flipped out. Cracked up. Went totally nuts!"

"But why?" I asked.

"Well," Monty said, "the articles I read said Lars just couldn't handle the pressure of the competition and everybody pinning all their hopes on him and everything. I think he ended up in a sanitarium for a while. As I remember, there was some talk of him making a comeback, but if he's teaching here now, I guess he's decided he couldn't hack it."

Astounded and appalled, I sank into the chintz chair and tried to soothe myself with my rhythmic rocking routine. I thought of Lars's twitching eyelid and shuddered. Monty tossed an M&M's up in the air and caught it in her mouth, a feat I've never been able to master. "You look like you just saw a ghost," she said. "But I don't see why. After all, now you know your instructor is really an accomplished skier."

"Now I know my instructor is really an accomplished lunatic!" I said. "You don't happen to remember exactly what form Lars's breakdown took, do you? I mean, did it involve sneaking into innocent damsels' rooms at night and pilfering their suitcases?"

Monty laughed. "I don't remember," she said. She chomped her last piece of candy and rubbed her flat stomach. "What time do they serve dinner in this tomb of a place, anyway?"

"Six o'clock." I glanced at my watch and saw that it was already almost five-thirty. Suddenly I remembered my promise to meet Bobby for hot chocolate and a talk about cracking the caper. I told Monty about the meeting, and she immediately began rummaging through her wildly messy suitcase for a change of clothes. While I wrestled a brush through my fuzzy hair, Monty went into the bathroom and turned on the water. A second later she came back out with soap all over her face.

"Weren't you going to tell me something before?" she asked. "Right before I fell out of that wardrobe thing?"

"That's right!" I said. I rescued the hairbrush from a particularly vicious tangle. The Lars Lundquist story had thrown me for such a loop, I'd totally forgotten my brilliant motive-theory breakthrough. But now, as Monty rinsed and toweled her face, I held forth on my subject.

"I realized this afternoon," I said, "that I've been looking at everything backward. I've been thinking about each single weird event and why it was done, instead of looking at the total effect of all the weird events put together!"

Monty stared at me over the top of her towel. "Well, go on!" she said impatiently. "What have you figured out about the total effect?"

"The motive!" I cried triumphantly. "Or anyway, part of the motive. Or at least I think it's part of the motive.

83

Maybe. The total effect of all the weird events has been to gum up the works, to make people scared, to drive guests away, basically, to interfere with the operations of Snowshoe Mountain Lodge!"

"You mean—" Monty began.

"Right!" I broke in. *"Someone is trying to sabotage this place!* It's as plain as the nose on your freshly-washed face. I should have figured it out before. I mean, first of all, we're only here because the lodge was offering bargain rates in the middle of the season. On the bus coming here, Bobby told me some friends of his left the lodge early because they thought it was haunted. And the first time I went into the lobby, some other guests were leaving in a huff and demanding a refund. Then Bobby announces to all the guests that someone got into his locked room, which I'm sure alarmed a lot of people. And my first reaction when my suitcase was stolen was to think about leaving. It's only normal!"

"But why?" Monty asked. "Why does someone want to sabotage business at Snowshoe?"

Well, that's the trouble with being a detective. No one stands around and pats you on the back for what you have figured out. All they do is ask you questions about what you *haven't* figured out! "I'm not sure about that part yet," I admitted reluctantly. "But now that we think we know why all this strange stuff is happening, we can concentrate on one thing: Who benefits from Snowshoe Mountain Lodge going down the tubes?"

I shot at glance at Monty to see if I'd impressed her with

my logic. "Amazingly enough," she said, "everything you've said makes a lot of sense. Assuming, that is, that the culprit is doing all this for a rational purpose, and that he's not just an uncomplicated psycho."

Well, that was a good point, but I chose not to think about it because it didn't fit in with my theory, and it made me more nervous than ever about living and skiing side by side with all the wackos I'd met at Snowshoe. Anyway, we were already late for my meeting with Bobby, so we didn't have any more chance to talk about the mystery right then. Freshly scrubbed and brushed, we locked our door and hurried through the dark, winding halls to the dining room. On the way I realized how hungry I was and gave Monty an enthusiastic description of the wonderful food at Snowshoe. "And tonight," I concluded, "we're supposed to have chocolate mousse torte."

When we got to the dining room, Bobby was nowhere to be found. "We're late," Monty pointed out. "Do you think he gave up on us?"

"I don't think so. He was dying to be a hotshot detective. I can't imagine him giving up so fast. He's probably just late. Let's go back through the halls and try to find him."

We left the lobby and started back through the creepy halls once again. There was no sign of Bobby, and I began to wonder if he'd had the nerve to forget about meeting me in the dining room. I turned to say something to Monty, but she put a hand on my arm. "Listen," she whispered.

I stood still and listened hard. "I don't hear any—" I began. But just then I did hear something. *Swish, clomp, thump. Swish, clomp, thump.* Whatever it was, it definitely was not the sound of normal human footsteps. But it definitely was right behind us—and getting closer by the minute.

13

"Ooooffff!" Bobby Berman dashed around the corner and almost crashed into us. A few days ago I would have felt like smacking him for his clumsiness, but now, as I peeled my body off the wall, I almost threw my arms around him. With his red face and panting body, Bobby looked refreshingly human.

I helped Monty up and started to say hello to Bobby. But he was staring at something over our shoulders. *Swish, clomp, thump* sounded one more time. Slowly, Monty and I turned around to face whatever ghastly apparition was behind us. Then we both laughed out loud with relief. There was no one behind us but Pixie, who smiled in response to our laughter and sneezed into one of her familiar green tissues.

It was then that I noticed Pixie's left leg. It was encased in a plaster cast! And she was supporting her shrimpy body on a pair of wooden crutches, which had undoubtedly been the source of the *thump* in the aforementioned *swish, clomp, thump* concert.

"What happened to you?" Bobby bellowed. "The last time I saw you, you and Lars were schussing down Suicide Run!"

Pixie shrugged and shook her pigtails ruefully. "I took one run too many, I guess, and had a bad fall. And you can see the results! Luckily, a departing guest was passing right by the hospital on his way home, so he drove me there and they put the cast on immediately. And it's only a minor fracture, so they let me have crutches instead of sticking me into a wheelchair."

Quick work, I thought. The local doctors must have had a lot of practice with broken bones, given all the ski slopes around here. A horrifying thought came to me. If the head of the ski school could fracture her leg, what were the chances for a dunce like me? "How did it happen, Pixie?" I asked.

"Well, I'm not exactly sure, to tell you the truth. Lars and I were checking the trails in the late afternoon— always the most dangerous time because of the shadows on the snow—when Lars stopped to adjust his bindings with one of those tools he always carries around. I went on ahead down Breakneck Pass, when all of a sudden some skier came rushing down behind me, wildly out of control. He must not have seen me, because he headed right at me and knocked me right off balance! I skidded off the trail and ended up wrapped around a tree. Frankly, I was lucky to escape with only a slight fracture!"

"That's terrible!" Monty said. "Did the skier stop to see if you were hurt? Did you see who it was?"

A bewildered look came over Pixie's perky face. "Well, it's odd," she said. "Even though it's a pretty warm day, the skier had a scarf over his face. Though in spite of that, I did think there was something familiar about him. Anyway, you can bet I'm going to keep my eyes open for anyone wearing a purple-and-white-striped scarf around here!"

I swallowed my indignant gasp and avoided looking at Monty. I knew we were both thinking the exact same thing. The scarf in my stolen suitcase was purple and white. And Pixie's accident sounded suspiciously like it had been no accident. Our felon was at it again.

"How did you get down the hill?" Bobby was asking Pixie.

"Oh, someone finally came along and found me lying there," she answered. "I don't know *what* became of Lars. I guess fixing his skis took him longer than he'd thought . . . or else he got lost in the dream world he lives in," she added with a laugh.

Bobby asked Pixie where she was going, since the dining room was in the other direction. She said she'd been hunting for her mislaid clipboard when she'd heard a funny noise in the kitchen and wondered if there could be a mouse in the cupboards. So Bobby insisted we should investigate (over my strong objections), but when we stuck our heads through the swinging side entrance to the kitchen, we didn't find or hear any form of rodent. I did find Pixie's clipboard on one of the countertops, however.

She was completely surprised when I handed it to her. She said she hadn't been anywhere near the kitchen that afternoon, and I decided the saboteur had undoubtedly added clipboard pilfering to his list of tricks.

We all went back into the dining room and helped ourselves to hot chocolate from the pot on the sideboard there. We'd just sat down at a table when shaggy-headed Lars Lundquist walked into the dining room. He came over to our table and said hello. Then he turned to Monty. "I do not believe I've had the pleasure of meeting you," he said.

"This is my cousin Monty Tierny, from Denver," I said hastily. "This is my ski instructor . . . well, that is, he's not just *my* instructor, but he teaches the beginners' class, which as you know I'm in. Anyway, his name's Lars Lundquist. But you already know that because you've heard of him before." It was my usual smooth introduction.

Lars said to Monty, "I am gratified there is still someone left on earth who remembers my brief career as a racer." I glanced sharply at him. Was his eyelid twitching again? It occurred to me that given Lars's past problems, he might not really be all that gratified to meet someone who remembered his history.

Pixie glanced at her watch and raised her eyebrows. "Aren't you three a bit early for dinner?" she asked. "Lars and I thought we'd have time to have a little meeting about some ski-school business poor Lars is handling because of my leg—now that I have my clipboard back, thanks to Kate!"

Never a great one for taking hints, Bobby pulled up a chair and sat down. "We're having a meeting, too, Henderson," he said to Pixie. Apparently, even acting heads of ski schools aren't exempt from being addressed by their last names. "About the case."

Pixie looked bewildered. "Case of *what*?" she asked.

"The case of all the strange stuff that's been happening around here," Bobby answered. "We plan to get to the bottom of it!"

Loopy Lars laughed lightly, but his eye twitched violently at the same instant. "Oh," he said, settling into a chair. "You mean you are going to track down our resident poltergeist?"

"Poltergeist, shmoltergeist!" Bobby boomed. "Clancy here has shot down that ghostly-legend stuff single-handed!"

Pixie and Lars both turned to stare at me, and I squirmed under their scrutiny. Then Pixie smiled her perky smile. "Well, I'll sleep better knowing that! I hope you track the culprit down, whatever it is!" She shook her pigtails. "This year is the first time anything like this has happened at Snowshoe Lodge, at least since I've been here. And that's a long time."

I grinned moronically, muttered something incoherent, and backed away from the table. The three of us sat down in a far corner and, while I drank hot chocolate, Monty told Bobby about my motive theory. I glanced out the window and noticed it was snowing. Bobby told me it had already been coming down heavily for a while. By then other guests had started arriving for dinner, and within fifteen minutes the big room was almost full. Annie and Ralph and Nita came in together, and we waved them over to our table. Soon Peter and his mother arrived, looking as if they were in the middle of their customary verbal sniping about who knows what. As they approached our table, they stopped talking to each other, and we all got up and shifted our seats so they'd have room to sit down with us.

When Lynda Dalton appeared in the doorway, I smirked, realizing there wouldn't be room for her to sit with us. But I hadn't reckoned on Lynda's gall. Darned if she didn't go to another table, beg their pardon, and swipe one of their extra place settings and chairs! Of course, we all had to scuffle our own chairs uncomfortably close so she could squeeze herself in. I was so squashed, I didn't see how I could possibly enjoy dinner.

Of course, when the food arrived, I immediately forgot all my troubles. Tonight we were having small, thick filet mignons wrapped in bacon and surrounded by crunchy roasted potatoes. As I broke open a hot, crispy roll, I noticed that somewhere during the course of the afternoon I'd managed to get some kind of powdery white junk all over my fingers. Discreetly, I stuck my hands under the table and rubbed them on my napkin.

For a while none of us talked at all. We just sat there, chewing, savoring, and swallowing. Soon, though, Peter turned to Monty and asked her where she'd learned to ski. Bobby was interested, too, and the three of them started comparing their favorite ski areas. Peter talked about how he wanted to become a ski racer, and in an instant the atmosphere at the table changed. As he went on and on enthusiastically about how he hoped to try out for the U.S. team, his mother stiffened in her chair and her mouth became such a thin line, it practically disappeared. You could almost see her struggling to maintain her self-control. But she finally lost the battle and started to talk.

"Skiing!" she said through her teeth. "You'd think it was the most important thing in the world! What about education? What about going to a good school and doing something significant with your life? I tell you, Peter, you think about skiing so much that sometimes I believe you'd do *anything* to succeed with it!"

Peter's happy look was immediately replaced by his usual expression of suppressed rage and suspicion. There was a tense, uneasy silence at the table; fortunately, the waitress's coming to clear away the dinner dishes broke the mood. I was particularly glad to see her since I was impatiently awaiting the arrival of the chocolate mousse torte.

At last little Camille came toward us, carrying a large covered tray. She put the tray down on our table and lifted the top. I was expecting the warm, earthy brown hue of chocolate mousse, so you can imagine my shock and dismay when I perceived that our dessert was green. Not only that, it was quivering. I blinked, hoping I'd gone temporarily snowblind. But a second glance told me my worst fears were true. The Snowshoe Lodge was serving Jell-O!

Camille dished up eight disgusting helpings, and then realized she was one bowl short, naturally, because she hadn't expected Lynda to push her way into our table. She turned to go back to the kitchen for another bowl. Before I could stop myself, I jumped up to follow.

I caught her just before she left the room. "Camille," I whispered, "what happened to the chocolate mousse torte?"

"The chocolate," Camille answered. "It disappeared from the kitchen this afternoon. Everything seems to disappear around here. Except for the jinx. That seems to be here to stay!"

14

No one ate the Jell-O except for Bobby, who apparently will eat anything. In fact, when he finished, he asked if he could have mine. I shoved my bowl toward him. I averted my eyes as the green stuff jiggled and dribbled its way to his mouth. Gag me with a ski pole.

Marsha, who'd been forbiddingly silent since her tirade about the value of higher education, finally pulled herself together enough to plaster on her ghastly smile and inform us that after dinner another movie would be shown in the front parlor. This time it was going to be a funny, old-fashioned skiing film that featured a lot of people tripping over their skis and falling down. Marsha assured me I'd split my sides laughing, so Monty and I decided to go.

Then Lynda turned to Peter and said she'd heard there was a Ping-Pong table in the basement and would he like to play a few games before it was time for the movie. Peter absentmindedly agreed, but, without batting a single one of his alluring, spiky black lashes, he turned to Monty and asked if she and I would like to play doubles with them. You could almost hear Lynda's pearly white teeth being ground down to tiny nubs.

Monty looked interested, so I shrugged and nodded, knowing that my cousin would probably bludgeon me with a blunt instrument if I said I didn't want to play. Bobby said he was too full of dinner to play, but he and Annie offered to come along and referee.

Somehow, by the time we got to the Ping-Pong room, Monty and Peter were already lined up on one side of the table, and I was stuck with Lynda for a partner. After five minutes of play the score was eighteen to three, and we only got those three because Peter kept trying to slam these unbelievably violent smashes that missed the end of the table and ricocheted off the walls. My cousin, who's always believed I should try harder at games, sighed loudly whenever I missed an easy shot. She'd already sighed about forty-two times when I gave up counting.

The lopsided score made it clear to everyone that we had to rearrange the teams, and for the second game I was paired with Monty—which she seemed to find even more annoying than having me as an opponent. With my cousin's skill we were actually able to give them a run for their money, but I was just too much of a handicap, and they beat us, twenty-one to seventeen. When they scored their twenty-first point, Lynda squealed and threw her arms around Peter's neck, like they'd won the Publisher's Clearinghouse Sweepstakes or something.

Appealingly flushed with victory, Lynda suggested playing another game, but Peter said he had to be getting back upstairs to set up the projector. Annie offered to take his place so we could play another game without him, but oddly enough, Lynda suddenly lost interest and said she had to go to her room for something—no big surprise, since she hadn't put on new mascara for at least five minutes.

Bobby said he'd now digested enough dinner to be able to play, but I said I had to run to the bathroom first. I left the recreation room and went down the basement hall till I found the little door marked "Ladies." It was stifling in the tiny room, so my first action on stepping inside was to go to the old, paint-peeling window and shove it open as far as I could—which, given the ancient state of the window frame, was about two inches. As I grappled with the window, I heard a loud backfire followed by a deep rumbling sound from outside. I decided some kind of behemoth delivery truck had just arrived at the lodge. As

I breathed in the cool air coming through the crack, I heard a new sound. *Padda, padda, padda*—like footsteps running across packed snow.

In a flash I was hunched over, peering out at the darkened night. The *padda, padda, padda* continued for half a second and then stopped, and with my usual faith in my senses, I immediately started wondering if I'd imagined the whole thing. Besides, even if I hadn't, I told myself, there were many legitimate reasons for someone to be running around in the dark outside the lodge. Like what? I asked myself. Well, like jogging! I answered triumphantly. Oh, sure, Clancy, I responded sarcastically. There's nothing like a late-night jog on top of six feet of icy snow.

Shut up! These stupid conversations with myself were getting me nowhere. In a distracted frame of mind, I left the bathroom and wandered back to the Ping-Pong room. I didn't feel like playing anymore, but Bobby insisted that he and Annie have a game of doubles against Monty and me. Because I was still brooding about the *padda, padda, padda*, my standard of play was even lower than my usual abysmal pit, and I hit my first five returns right off the end of the table. I barely noticed. But then a loud *THWACK* reverberated throughout the basement, and I almost had a heart attack on the spot. Startled, I looked questioningly at Monty. She was glaring at me. All at once I realized that she had caused the thwack herself by slamming the paddle down on top of the table. "You may have your mind on other things, Kate," she said through her teeth, "but some of us are trying to play Ping-Pong!"

A red-hot flush rushed to my cheeks. I was too embarrassed even to glance at Bobby and Annie. My cousin was talking to me like I was a four-year-old! "It's only a game, Monty," I began angrily. "And you know I'm not very good at it."

"The reason you're not very good is that you don't pay any attention to what you're doing! And I for one have had enough of it!" With another *thwack*, Monty slammed her paddle down on the table and stormed out of the room. I was so mortified that for a few seconds I couldn't move. Then kindly Bobby Puffbear rescued me by saying it was just about time for the movie to start. Blinking back self-pitying tears, I followed him and Annie out of the room. But when we got back upstairs, there was some kind of commotion going on. The front door of the hotel was wide open, and people were standing around in the lobby looking worried.

While Bobby and Annie stopped to talk to Marsha Shade, I wormed my way over to the front door and peered out, trying to get a glimmering of what was going on. Just then Ralph Nickerson came in from outside. His thick, white hair was so windblown, it stood out from his face like a lion's mane. I asked him what had happened, but he didn't seem to hear me, so I touched his arm and repeated my question. "What happened, Ralph? What's going on?"

"I'm not sure," he said. His normally hearty insurance-salesman's voice was vague and distracted.

"But why is everyone standing around like this? Why are the doors open?"

The sound of my voice finally seemed to register on Ralph, and he gave a little start. "Oh, hi there, Kate," he said in his usual jovial tones. "Why, we've had an avalanche, of course! Didn't you hear the boom?"

My mouth dropped open. "I didn't hear a thing. . . ." I began. "But maybe the driver of the delivery truck did. He must have been outside when the avalanche happened."

Ralph gripped my arm with surprisingly strong fingers. "What truck?" he demanded. "What are you talking about? *What did you see?*"

I gaped at him, too dumbfounded to speak. Ralph's hearty manner had suddenly vanished. His voice was fierce and aggressive, his mild gray gaze piercing and intense. To my amazement and dismay, he began pulling me across the lobby toward the front parlor. As we neared the entrance, I saw Pixie leaning on her crutches near the parlor door. My expression must have shown my fear, because when she saw me, a look of surprise and concern came over her unusually flushed face. She started to hobble toward us, but before she got more than a few steps, Ralph had pushed open the parlor door and hauled me inside.

"We can talk in here," he began. Then he broke off abruptly as he took in the state of the front parlor. "What the heck?" he said. The temperature in the big room was well below freezing, and the reason why was obvious. One of the large French windows was wide open, and the cold wind was howling into the building.

As Ralph hurried over to the window, I realized I was at least temporarily forgotten. As quickly and quietly as I could, I slipped back out the door and rejoined the people in the lobby. Frantically, I scanned the crowd for familiar faces. I was desperate to tell someone about Ralph's strange behavior.

Finally, I spotted Annie and Bobby over by the desk. I hurried across the lobby to them. Just then I realized that Monty was standing right next to them. "Wow, Bobby!" she was saying as I approached. "An avalanche! I've been skiing a million times, but I've never been so close to an avalanche before!"

"I have," Bobby answered. He launched into an interminable story about his trip to Squaw Valley three years ago. I made several attempts to interrupt and tell all of them about Ralph Nickerson, but no one would listen to me. Just when I finally got their attention, the front door of the lodge blew open once again. First Lars came in, closely followed by brooding Peter. Then Ted Tedley, the owner of Clementine's, arrived carrying about half a ton of snow on the shoulders of his parka. He brushed it off onto our feet.

"The avalanche has completely buried the road between the two lodges," he said in his bullfrog voice. "Clementine's is okay. We can still get up and down the mountain. But Snowshoe is another story. You're completely cut off up here. And all the phone lines are down as well."

15

Everyone was lounging around, acting as if nothing was happening, but I could tell I wasn't the only one who was worried. People were trying to carry on casual conversations, but somehow the words were tense and speeded up, like a song by the Chipmunks. I kept looking around for Grand Inquisitor Ralph Nickerson, wondering when he'd realize I'd left before he could interrogate me. I must have slipped his mind, though, because after a while I saw him come out of the parlor and stride away without so much as a glance in my direction.

About fifteen minutes later Marsha Shade came into the lobby and announced they were going to go ahead and show the movie as they'd originally planned. She spoke in her false, too-bright, hotel-staff voice, but her face looked more strained than ever. As she talked, her eyes scanned the crowd and finally came to rest on her son, whom she scrutinized with an intense black gaze that perfectly matched the laser-beam look he was giving her.

Most of the people in the lobby wandered in to the front parlor, where the windows had been closed and the temperature was almost back up to normal. I thought I had too many worries on my mind to enjoy the movie, but in fact it was just what I needed. The film started out showing all these old-fashioned idiots dressed in knickers and stocking caps tripping over their ancient six-mile-long wooden skis. Then it showed some *modern* idiots wearing Bogner overalls and tripping over their new, streamlined short skis. It was so funny that by the end, in spite of everything, I was almost able to delude myself into thinking I was having a normal, enjoyable vacation in the mountains.

That normal feeling lingered after the end of the movie—for about two seconds. When the lights went back on, I blinked, glanced around, and almost drowned in self-pity as all my anxieties flooded back. The big parlor looked like a set from *Night of the Living Dead.* At the back of the room Peter and Marsha Shade were rewinding the film in zombied-out, Dracula-eyed silence. Camille was standing—or, more accurately, swaying—by ugly Ted Tedley, just inside the door. From her semidemented expression I could tell she'd regressed to her original state of dazed hysteria. Lars and Pixie were both out in the lobby. Pixie's poor nostrils were redder than Rudolph's nose, giving her the appearance of someone who'd just run a marathon through a snowbank. Lars was compulsively fiddling with the medals around his neck, and even from this distance I could see that his eyelid was twitching like a metronome.

There was no sign of Ralph Nickerson, though Nita was knitting in a chair only a few feet away. But who knew where he was? He might be lurking around in some darkened hallway, waiting for his chance to haul me off again.

Of course, none of this was as bad as the fact that Monty and I were barely talking to each other. When all the guests left the parlor, the two of us trailed out with them. Still without speaking, we headed through the halls to our room and started getting ready for bed. When we had to say something, we were polite—a sure sign that something was wrong between us. I kept waiting for Monty to break the ice, but she can be a total stoneface when she wants to. By the time I'd finished brushing and flossing, I was on the verge of tears.

Totally miserable, I came out of the bathroom and started pawing around under my pillow for my nightgown. My searching fingers touched something bumpy and crinkly wrapped up inside the fuzzy flannel. I opened up the nightie and pulled out a bag of peanut M&M's. All was forgiven.

When I turned around, Monty was sitting on her bed, biting open her own bag. "Did you bring a truckload of these, or what?" I asked her. "You never seem to run out."

Monty laughed. "You are some detective," she said. "There's a vending machine downstairs in the Ping-Pong room. I raced out and bought some while you were in the bathroom performing your nightly oral surgery on yourself."

"Great timing," I said, tossing candy into my mouth. "After I eat this, I'll have to go through the whole routine again." Neither of us said anything about our scene in the basement, because we each knew the other one was sorry. Then Monty brought up a new subject. "Listen. I think maybe we should go home—or else see if we can get reservations at another ski area. This mystery business isn't funny anymore."

"I know. That Jell-O at dinner was the last straw."

"I was thinking more about Pixie's 'accident,'" Monty said. "And the avalanche."

"The avalanche!" I repeated in surprise. "What does that have to do with the mystery?"

Monty's slender face was thoughtful. "Well, if you know what you're doing," she began, "you can cause an avalanche on purpose. The more I think about it, the more I think that might be what happened tonight."

Suddenly I sat bolt upright. "Oh, my gosh!" I cried. "The backfire. The one I heard in the bathroom! It could have been a cannon going off outside! And the rumbling sound might not have been a truck at all. It might have been the avalanche!"

Monty gaped at me. Then she nodded. "That clinches it," she said. "If you heard a cannon boom, then the avalanche was deliberate. But you shouldn't be so surprised, Kate. After all, it fits right in with your sabotage theory. Now business here is completely disrupted. The phone lines are down. The road is blocked. No buses can get up the mountain with more skiers. And no food or supplies, either."

"But we could all have been buried alive!" I said.

"I know," Monty said. "That's why I think we should

leave. I think this 'prankster' of yours is going off the deep end. Until now he or she has been pulling off silly little tricks like swiping suitcases and cutting lift-ticket wires—"

"Don't forget the chocolate."

"And snitching chocolate. And pretending to be a poltergeist—"

"You know, I had an idea about that today!" I interrupted excitedly. "I think the fake ghost was the one who started a rumor that there was a legend about Snowshoe Mountain Lodge being haunted. I mean Camille said she'd never heard anything about it in all the years her uncle owned this place. But then, all of a sudden this year, everyone seemed to be talking about the *old* story. It struck me that, somehow, the prankster planted the idea to make people reluctant to come here!"

"I bet you're right. But now I think the imposter ghost has decided that the haunted-ski-lodge idea wasn't working well enough. Look at what he's been doing lately. Today, if our suspicions are correct, he pushed the acting head of the ski school right into a tree! And he just might have been responsible for the avalanche, which put a whole lot of people in real danger. The ski patrols plan their mini-avalanches very carefully, working as a team. It seems to me that one person working alone and at night could have made a mistake pretty easily. If things had gone wrong, one of the lodges could have been buried. People could have been killed!"

I felt the blood draining from my face. "Monty," I whispered, "I'm almost sure I heard the culprit tonight. When I was in the bathroom in the basement, I heard the sound of someone running across the snow. It must have been *him* leaving the scene of the crime!" I thought for a minute longer. "What if," I went on slowly, "he saw me looking out the window? And maybe he thinks I saw him? I didn't, of course. But how would he know that?"

A look of real concern came over my cousin's face. "Now I really think we'd better go home!"

"We can't go home, Monty! The road down the mountain has been cut off. And the phones are dead. We can't even call the police!"

For a chilling moment we stared at each other. "All right then," Monty said calmly. "We simply have to solve the mystery ourselves." She scratched her fluffy head. "You're the one who reads all those mystery books, Kate. What would one of your detectives do in a situation like this?"

I reached over and opened the drawer of the little night table between our beds. I pulled out a pencil and a pile of hotel stationery. "Make a list of suspects," I said. "They always do that."

Well, for the next hour we slaved over our list. The first thing we decided was that the prankster almost had to be someone who worked at Snowshoe Lodge. Camille had said the dirty tricks had been going on all ski season, so only staff members would have had the opportunity.

"Except," Monty said, "for Ted Tedley. And those people in your class from Phoenix. You said they'd been here for two months."

"Ralph and Nita Nickerson," I said. Then I described Ralph's total personality change in the front parlor. "At first he was his usual ho-ho-ho self. But he started acting really weird when I mentioned hearing what I thought was a delivery truck outside. Maybe he had something to do with the avalanche and thought I was a witness."

"Put him on the list!" Monty ordered.

"Yes, master!" I said, scribbling furiously.

When we were finally finished with our labors, our list of suspects included Ted Tedley, Ralph and Nita Nickerson, Camille Higonnet, Lars Lundquist, Pixie Henderson, Marsha Shade, and her son, Peter. We went over each person and tried to figure out a motive for him or her.

"Well, Ted Tedley has an obvious motive," Monty said. "If he puts Snowshoe out of business, everyone will have to ski at Sunburst and stay at Clementine's, and he'll make a bundle."

"I think he's a little *too* obvious. In mysteries the person with the most to gain almost never commits the crime."

"This isn't a book, Kate! But still, you may be right. I think Marsha Shade is the bad guy. She's the hotel bookkeeper, after all. She's probably been fiddling with the accounts and wants to put the lodge out of business before she's discovered."

I made a few notes next to Marsha's name. "I don't know about that," I said slowly. "But I do think she doesn't trust her son and he doesn't trust her. It has something to do with his going off last year before he'd finished high school." I studied our list and frowned. "You went out of order, Monty," I complained. "What about Ralph and Nita Nickerson? Ralph was certainly acting strange tonight. But what could his motive be?"

Monty thought for a minute. "You know," she said at last, "we really don't know anything about any of these people. I mean, Ralph could really be the representative for a big evil capitalistic corporation that wants to drill an oil well on this land."

"Or he could really be a homicidal schizophrenic," I added with a shudder, vividly recalling his viselike grip on my arm. I put a big question mark by the Nickersons' name and moved down the list. "I don't know why we put Camille on here," I said. "She's the only one who couldn't possibly have a motive for hurting business at Snowshoe Mountain Lodge. She's the owner!"

"Hmmm," Monty said. "She's also a great skier and seems to really care about the lodge. But she does take all those pills. Who knows what she might do under their influence?" She chewed the end of the pencil. Then she made a face and reached for her last M&M's. "Isn't there some kind of insurance you can take out on your own business or something? In case it fails? Maybe you could find out from Ralph. Isn't he an insurance salesman?"

"He claims to be," I said, staring at Camille's name. I was remembering all the things she'd told me about her uncle Jacques and her problems at the lodge. It had sounded genuine to me. But had it been a lie—or, even more frightening, a hallucination?

Monty came over to see the other names on the list. "Lars," she read. "And Pixie."

"Well, even though Lars is a wonderful ski instructor, we know he's had mental problems. Maybe he's flipping out again."

"What about Pixie? She might have some kind of grudge against Camille that we don't know about, maybe something to do with ski-school politics? Or else maybe she's wormed her way into Camille's affections and figures prominently in Camille's will and is trying to drive her to suicide? Don't you think she's just a little too cute to be true? I mean, please spare me those pigtails and that perky smile!"

"And that broken leg, which has put her almost totally out of commission!" I said, heatedly rising to Pixie's defense. "You don't have to be so cynical just because someone's cuter than you are. I think Pixie's nice!"

"*Too* nice," Monty began. "She . . ." She took a look at my angry face and broke off, realizing we were on the verge of another fight. "Oh, well," she sighed. "I guess her broken leg rules her out, so we might as well stop arguing about her. But this discussion is all pretty useless anyway. We just don't know enough about these people."

"You're right," I said, happy to agree about something. "It's too bad we don't have more information to work with."

Monty didn't say anything, but when I turned to look at her, her expression had become intense and excited. She rubbed her hands together. "You've put your finger right on the problem!" she said. "We have to search for clues."

Without realizing what I was doing, I started wringing my fingers, like some kind of poor, threatened heroine in an old melodrama. "You don't actually mean . . ." I began nervously.

"Yes, I do," Monty replied. She glanced at her watch. "We'll wait another hour or so. Until everyone is asleep. Then we'll sneak out of here and hunt for some evidence."

"But what if someone catches us?" I asked. My croaking voice was worthy of Ted Tedley.

"That's easy. We'll just say we're going down to the vending machine for more M&M's."

Oh, well. As I've frequently pointed out, there's no point in arguing with my cousin once she's made up her mind. Anyway, getting more M&M's wasn't a bad idea, because we were both cleaned out. We settled down on our beds to wait. At exactly one A.M. we opened our door and tiptoed out into the darkened hallway.

16

As stealthily as possible we crept along the guestroom hallways and down the three steps to the lobby. Without hesitating, Monty made a beeline for the office. I yanked at the sleeve of her sweater.

"Where do you think you're going?" I asked.

"To get the master key so we can search the rooms tomorrow while everyone's skiing. It's the only way we can get the goods on the prankster."

I couldn't believe my ears. *Get the goods on the prankster,* indeed! Monty was starting to sound exactly like Bobby. But worse than that, she was actually planning to steal the master key and break into all the rooms in the hotel!

My fearless cousin ducked behind the front desk and reached for the office doorknob. Just in time I saw the light coming out from the crack under the door. I grabbed Monty's arm and pulled her back. We stood stock-still, holding our breath. Then Monty got down on her knees and peered through the keyhole.

A few seconds later she moved sideways and motioned for me to have a look. I couldn't see anything but my own eyelashes, but then I saw the top of a gray head bent over some papers on the big, cluttered desk. The person glanced up, and I recognized Marsha Shade's anxious black eyes.

The bookkeeper shifted some papers, and I smashed my eye against the keyhole, straining to see what she was doing. I felt Monty's fingers clutch my shoulder. Irritably, I tried to shrug off her hand. But she merely tightened her hold. Suddenly she was yanking me away from the door.

"What do you think you're . . . ?" I began angrily. As I looked up, I swallowed hard and completely lost my voice. It seemed I'd made a little mistake. The hand on my shoulder wasn't Monty's after all. It was Peter Shade's. My loyal cousin was nowhere to be seen.

If I had thought Peter looked slightly sinister before, he now looked positively satanic. In the shadowy lobby, his face was almost literally black with rage. He put both hands on my shoulders and gripped hard. "What's the meaning of this?" he hissed.

I swallowed again and tried to speak. "I was just . . . uh . . . that is, we wanted to . . . um, you know, investigate . . ." My voice trailed off.

I must have looked kind of pathetic, because Peter loosened his hold on me. "Listen," he said in an intense whisper, "you're only here for a week, and in a few days you'll forget all about this place and your 'investigating.' But we live here. We can solve our own problems. So stop messing around with what doesn't concern you! Or you might regret the consequences!" He glared at me with his unearthly eyes, released his grip, and stalked out of the lobby.

I stood right where I was, shaking like the proverbial leaf. Suddenly I heard a new hissing sound behind me. I swayed and almost fell over. Had Peter come back to make good his threat about "consequences"?

But this time it wasn't Peter. It was Monty, and she was breathing hard and *smiling*. I wanted to strangle her, but before I could make my lunge, she started chattering in an enthusiastic whisper.

"Look what I found!" she said. "A clue to beat all clues!" She held out her hand, and in my curiosity to see what she'd found, I momentarily forgot my anger. I peered at the object she was holding, and I caught my breath. It was my purple-and-white-striped scarf, the very one Pixie said her assailant on the slopes had been wearing.

Monty pointed toward the front of the lobby. "One of the lockers was a tiny bit open," she began. "There's some other stuff in there, too. And—" She stopped short as we both heard the sound of footsteps coming along the guest room hall. Quick as a flash Monty was slithering along the wall, heading in the direction of the sound.

I decided it was less terrifying to follow her than to stay by myself in the shadows, so I tiptoed after her. She headed up the steps and started prowling along the hallway near the rooms where Camille and some of the other staff lived. We couldn't hear the footsteps anymore, but Monty kept right on going. I wondered if my cousin had any plan of action whatsoever, or if she was just behaving the way she thought a detective was supposed to behave.

Suddenly she skidded to a stop and pointed to a piece of snow on the carpet. "Someone's been outside recently," she whispered dramatically. No kidding, I said to myself.

But then I remembered the wet footprints in my room the night my suitcase had disappeared. Was this a clue? Would someone who lived in the lodge need to keep leaving snowy deposits everywhere?

Monty bent down to examine her find. Maybe she had some notion of trying to lift fingerprints off the sodden lump. As I watched her, I was overcome by a massive yawn, and suddenly became aware of my state of complete exhaustion. The mental and physical strain of the last day hit me, right in the sleep zone, and I felt as if I were about to keel over on the spot. I decided I couldn't care less if the prankster transported Snowshoe Mountain Lodge to the outer moons of Saturn, as long as I got a chance to lie down.

I yawned again and leaned my weary body against the wall. For a few blissful seconds I closed my eyes. But, to my awakening horror, my support slowly began to cave in behind me! I wasn't leaning against the wall at all, but against a closed door instead. And now someone was opening it!

With my mouth gaping wide in a silent scream, I fell backward, flailing my arms in a vain effort to catch my balance. But it was no use. *Whomp!* I slammed painfully onto the floor. An enormous shape loomed over my helpless head.

"Holy Toledo, Clancy!" a familiar voice boomed out. "What the heck are *you* doing out here in the hall in the middle of the night?"

17

I scrambled to my feet as Monty lunged forward and clapped a hand over Bobby's mouth. "Keep your voice down!" she commanded him. He rolled his eyes and nodded obediently. For once I was grateful for my cousin's field-marshal abilities.

"Whose room is that, Bobby?" I asked, pointing to the doorway he'd just exited. "What were you doing in there?"

"I'm not sure." His whisper, if you could call it that, was still pretty loud, but he was making an effort. "I couldn't sleep, so I decided to do a little investigating. When I came down this hall, I noticed the door was a little bit open, so I went inside to check the place out."

Before I could respond, Monty was circling behind us and slipping through the open doorway into the room. Bobby followed her in, and I, much more reluctantly, trailed after them. There I found the two of them opening drawers and peering under the bed as if they had some idea of what they were doing.

"Come on, you guys," I muttered. "Let's get out of here." Neither one of the would-be detectives bothered to glance at me. Nervously, I gazed around the room, wondering who lived there. I became aware of the number of posters taped up on the walls. All of them showed ski racers and jumpers in wild, contorted positions.

Then I noticed a long, thin black object lying across the corner of the bed. In the dark it was difficult to see what it was, so I crossed the room and touched the thing. My fingers felt cool metal and several heavy objects: a hammer, pliers, wrench, screwdriver, and a pair of wire cutters. The object was a tool belt. I had a clear memory of seeing it buckled around Peter Shade's waist. Later he'd said it had disappeared, but now it seemed to be back in his possession. Because there was no question in my mind that this was Peter's room. If I'd had any doubts, they were immediately zapped when I saw his fringed black-leather vest hanging over one of the bedposts, not to mention the ski-poster wallpaper. Those pictures had to be his. After all, didn't everyone say that Peter was obsessed with leaving Snowshoe and joining the pro racing circuit, even if it had to be over his mother's dead body?

Suddenly I was terrified. My shoulders still hurt from Peter's digging, threatening grip, and I didn't think I would ever forget the expression of murderous rage on his face. "I'm getting out of here!" I announced to my still-snooping compatriots. "You idiots can do what you want!"

To my surprise the idiots shrugged and docilely followed me out the door, like a pair of Mary's lambs. I was hoping they'd come to their so-called senses and realized we were in over our heads. But when I turned in the direction of our own room, Monty grabbed my arm and held out the purple-and-white-striped scarf she still clutched in her hands. "The locker," she reminded me. "We have to check out the other stuff."

She bounded off before anyone could stop her, with her faithful stooge Bobby hot on her heels. I hated to go along, but I had to admit I was curious about the locker and what was in it.

In the lobby I found Bobby and Monty gleefully hauling objects out of a large open locker. First they pulled out a toolbox. Then they pulled out two rectangular boxes, wrapped in gold-and-white paper with lettering on the outside. Finally they pulled out a leather suitcase. One look told me it was my dad's.

Bobby was hunched over the two rectangular boxes, trying to read what was written on the outside. "Hey!" he said in his normal voice. "This is the missing chocolate from dinner!"

I approached the locker and peered through the darkness at the number on the door, though in fact I didn't really need to see it. I was positive I remembered which locker this was. Number 13, Lars Lundquist's home away from home.

Even though I'd told Monty that Lars was a logical suspect, I guess I hadn't really thought it was true. For one thing, he'd been such a kindly, patient ski instructor, it was hard to believe he was really a criminal. But all this evidence certainly was damaging.

I didn't know what to think. But I did know my little inner voice was trying to tell me something. I needed to get out of this dark, spooky lobby so I could hear myself think.

Without saying anything, I reached for my suitcase and

turned to leave. Bobby hoisted up the boxes of chocolate. "We might as well put these back in the kitchen," he began. He broke off abruptly, and the three of us froze. We'd all heard the sound at the same instant. Someone was opening the lodge door from the outside. The cavern-like lobby was so huge, there was no time to run away to the hall. We were about to be discovered.

18

We barely had time to grab up the stuff on the floor and plaster ourselves against the wall behind a couch. As we stood, carved in stone like a mini Mount Rushmore, the big front doors opened and a dark figure stepped into the lobby. I couldn't see who it was, but the person passed in front of a window and his squat, stocky shape was silhouetted against the dim light. The midnight visitor was Ted Tedley.

I was dead certain Mr. Tedley would discover us, lurking in the shadows. But instead, he passed right through the lobby and on up the steps to the guest rooms. When he was gone, the three of us heaved a joint sigh of relief. I stirred and stretched my cramped muscles, wondering at old Ted's familiarity with Snowshoe Lodge. Even though it was one A.M., he hadn't been acting very clandestine.

When we were sure the coast was clear, I grabbed Dad's

suitcase and we scurried like rats through a maze in and out among the spooky, twisty hallways that led back to our room. Back in Room 13 we locked the door and tried to breathe normally. Monty and I threw ourselves onto our beds, and Bobby overflowed into the chintz rocking chair. In our haste to escape from the lobby, we'd neglected to put the chocolate back in the kitchen, and Bobby was still clutching a box under each arm. As I looked at him, I felt a special pang of pity. Tonight must have been a particular strain on him. Never before had Mouth Berman been forced to be so quiet for so long!

For a while we didn't say anything, but at last Bobby broke the silence. "I wonder how we can find out who uses locker number thirteen," he said.

"You can ask me," I answered. "It's Lars Lundquist. He told our class he always leaves his stuff in there."

Bobby's and Monty's eyes bugged out at me, and Bobby rubbed his hands together and chortled. "Well, then we've got our man!" he said. "Lundquist did it! I've cracked the case after only one night on the job!"

Even though I'd started thinking of Bobby as a friend, I still hadn't developed an immunity to his obnoxious out-bursts. I was about to roll my eyes at Monty when I realized she was nodding in agreement with what he'd said. "Lars must be cracking up again," she said. "He probably doesn't even know what he's doing!"

"We can't finger him to the fuzz," Bobby said out of the left side of his mouth, "since the phones are on the blink. I guess we'll have to go to Camille first thing in the morning."

"Right," Monty said. "She's the one in charge here, and—"

"Wait a minute, you two!" I broke in. "Aren't you getting a little bit ahead of yourselves here? We still don't know for sure that Lars is guilty. What evidence do we have?"

Monty's and Bobby's eyes bugged out again, this time in disbelief. "Your purple-and-white-striped scarf," Monty said at last, with exaggerated patience. "The chocolate, and *your own suitcase*! Isn't that obvious evidence?"

"Aha!" I shouted. "That's just it! It's *too* obvious. I mean, look at the situation. We—that is you, Bobby—announce to the whole world that we plan to get to the bottom of the case, and only a few hours later we 'happen' to discover a locker simply bursting with evidence. And not only that, it conveniently 'happens' to be partway open." I whirled around and faced my cousin. "And unless I miss my guess, my missing scarf just 'happened' to be sticking partway out so you couldn't fail to notice it, right, Monty?"

My cousin didn't answer me, but from the set of her shoulders I knew my sudden insight had been correct. Excited by my own brilliance, I paced around the room, ending up at the windows. I lifted the heavy curtain and stared out at the modern condominiums behind the lodge. "I mean, Lars may be nuts," I said, "but he's not a total idiot. Besides, I looked into that locker at lunchtime today. There was a lot of stuff in there—but no suitcase."

Well, Bobby and Monty finally admitted I'd made a good point (a frame-up might just be in the cards, according to Bobby), and they agreed not to turn Lars in tomorrow morning. We talked about the mystery a little more, trying to decide who might want to get Lars in trouble, but we concluded we were all so tired, we weren't getting anywhere. We decided we should go to bed and see if we felt any more intelligent in the morning.

Bobby left with the chocolate, saying he'd return it to the kitchen before going back to his room. When he was gone, I pushed the chintz chair up against our door. Then we crawled into bed in our clothes. For the first time in my life I neglected to brush and floss after eating sweets.

I was tired the next morning, but I had the thrill of putting on some fresh clothes from my recovered suitcase. Ted Tedley arrived at breakfast and announced that a work crew was on the way, but that the road probably wouldn't be clear for one day at least. I wondered out loud how *he* was able to keep popping in and out of the lodge if the road from Clementine's was blocked, but Annie told me she'd seen him arrive on a pair of snowshoes.

As I ate, I glanced around the dining room, wondering how to act when I encountered Peter Shade. Since I couldn't see him anywhere, I had at least a temporary reprieve. I did see Lynda Dalton holding court at a table with Darwin and his fawning friends from Valley High. I wondered if she'd finally given Peter up as a lost cause. I knew I had. After my scene with him last night, I never wanted to gaze into those black eyes again.

When we were finished with our eggs and bacon, Bobby, Monty, and I had a brief whispered conversation during which we decided we should go ahead to our respective ski lessons and keep our eyes peeled for clues. Half an hour later I was buckled into my boots and standing on my skis next to Lynda and the other beginners at the bottom of Powderpuff. Lars was telling us we were going to take our first ride on the Sunnyside chair lift. Everyone else in the class oohed and aahed with excitement, but I had my usual reaction—mortal terror. As we slipped and slid our way over to the lift line, I imagined all the things that could go wrong. The cable that held up the moving chairs could snap, and I could fall down and fracture my leg, just like Pixie. The engine that ran the lift could malfunction, and I could be left hanging in the wind, forty feet above the ground, slowly starving to death. The person next to me on the chair could turn out to be the Snowshoe saboteur, who would decide I "knew too much" and had to be eliminated.

In fact, of course it didn't turn out to be all that bad. I was a little upset when I realized they wouldn't actually stop the chair when it was time for me to sit on it, but that instead I'd have to ski up and stand on a little red dot while the moving seat rushed up behind me and banged into the back of my knees. I was sure I'd fall down and be decapitated, but in the end Annie and I both got on like real pros. Nosy Ralph Nickerson wasn't there, for which I was eternally grateful.

Anyway, I was doing okay with the chair lift until it was time to ski off the chair at the top of the hill. Once again the stupid thing never stopped. We were supposed to simply stand up, push off the chair, and glide effortlessly down a steep little path. Well, I stood up and pushed off, all right. But then the tips of my skis crossed, and I fell right in front of Annie, who naturally tripped over me and lost both her skis. Hopelessly tangled together, we slid down the path and stopped in a snowbank, a writhing, kicking mass of arms and legs. When I brushed off my face, I saw that they'd had to stop the lift so they could clear away the carnage we'd left in our path—skis, poles, hats, and Lynda Dalton, and little Nita Nickerson.

Lars skied over to me and helped me up. "Don't feel bad," he said. "Everyone falls off the chair the first time they try, though perhaps not quite so dramatically." He looked down at my feet in concern. "Kate," he said, "I am worried about the binding adjustment on your skis. They really should have released when you fell, the same way Annie's did. If your ski doesn't come off when your ankle twists, you could end up with a bad sprain or break."

He skied over to Nita and got my other pole. Then he came back to me. "When we reach the bottom, I want you to go into the ski shop and have them readjust the binding," he said. "I would do it myself here, but I did not have a chance to stop by my locker and pick up my tools this morning."

Dismayed, I glanced down at my feet. Suddenly my ankles seemed incredibly precious to me and as fragile as fine china. I was reluctant to jeopardize them by putting them through the contortions of ski class on a pair of defective skis. "Can't I go down ahead and get the bindings fixed right away?" I asked.

"Do you wish to take your skis off and walk?"

I remembered yesterday's fiasco when I'd tried to carry my skis. "If you show me the easiest way down, I'm sure I can ski it. I go so carefully, I fall over in slow motion. My ankles almost never twist."

Lars thought for a minute, rubbing his manly chin with his gloved hand. "Well, if it makes you nervous to participate in the class, I guess you could go on ahead if you go slowly," he said. He pointed off to the right. "The easiest possible trail is over there. In fact, it is not really a trail at all, but more of an open road. If you follow the big green circle signs, you should reach the bottom with no trouble."

I knew from my trail map that the big green circles designated easiest trails, while green squares meant intermediate. Threatening black diamond shapes stood for the expert slopes.

Feeling incredibly brave, I started off in the direction in which Lars had pointed. The trail, reassuringly named Baby Way, was more like a wide, gently sloping road than a trail. I assumed my wedge position and went slowly,

slowly down the middle. Of course, I fell down sometimes. But as I'd promised, I was going at such a snail's pace, I didn't fall very hard.

A deceptively easy-looking trail named Death Valley Run branched off down the mountain to the left. I shuddered as I saw the ominous black diamond that stood for an expert run and carefully kept myself way over to the right side of Baby Way. After a few minutes of easy skiing, I was feeling pretty cocky and started practicing my turns, trying to remember everything Lars, Bobby, and Monty had said the day before. For the first time I felt some slight control over my legs and feet.

Then I stopped cold and blinked my eyes. Baby Way had suddenly been transformed into another trail. A sign under a pine tree said its name was "Child's Play." Beside the name was the friendly green Easiest symbol. But to me the trail looked anything but easy. To me it looked exactly like a cliff.

19

"Okay, Kate," I said in an attempt at reassurance. "They wouldn't label a trail "Child's Play" unless it was easy, right? All you have to do is get over these huge, mean-looking bumps, and you'll come to the part that's easiest, right?"

Wrong! I screamed back at myself. After standing around at the top of the hill, hoping someone in a helicopter might spot me, I finally worked up the courage to slide my skis out onto one of the moguls at the top of Child's Play. I glanced down the hill and my head started spinning. There was no bumpy hard part at the beginning of the trail. The whole *slope* was a bumpy hard part!

In an instant I made up my mind. There was no way I was going to ski down that trail. I'd take off my skis and walk down the side of the mountain if it took me all day. I bent over to release the catch on my bindings, and that's when I made my fatal mistake. With my usual grace I lost my balance and started flapping my arms in the air. The next thing I knew, my skis had started forward and I was careening wildly down the slope.

Frantically, I fought to get control of my feet long enough to stop myself. But it was no use. My skis had taken on a life of their own. Screaming like a maniac, I *boing*ed from bump to bump, my body lurching forward and backward and then forward again as I bounced down the trail. I felt exactly like one of those little balls bashing around inside a pinball game.

My purple hat blew off and my hair whipped out around my head. But though I was scared, I hadn't completely given up hope. Sooner or later something had to slow me down. I prayed it wouldn't be one of the enormous evergreens waiting along the side of the trail.

At last I fell over onto my side, and I thought I'd stop for sure. Incredibly, I kept on moving, sliding and bashing my way down the mountain. I hit one more bump, and suddenly I was launched off the ground. I closed my eyes, and glided through the air like some kind of giant vampire bat. Then I landed on my face and sank about three feet into a bed of snow.

I was sure I'd been buried alive, but when I turned my head sideways, I could see branches and blue sky above me. I tried to flip over onto my back, but found that I was wedged so deeply into the snow, I could only move the top half of my body. My legs and feet *had* been buried alive.

By twisting my neck around, I was able to see that I was in some kind of pit of snow in the woods off the side of Child's Play. No one skiing on the trail would even be able to see me. I could lie out there all day and never be discovered. I felt desperately sorry for myself, but I couldn't even start crying. If I did, the tears would probably freeze on my face.

There was only one thing to do, and that was dig myself out. I pushed my body as far up as it would go and began scooping up pawfuls of snow and tossing them over my shoulder. It was hard work, but I kept at it. Ten minutes later I'd made such little progress that I really did start to cry. Just then I heard voices coming from the trail.

"Help!" I screamed at the top of my lungs. "HELP! Over here in the woods!"

For a minute I thought no one had heard me, but then I heard the scrootch of approaching skis. Soon a head appeared over the edge of my pit, and a large face blotted out the sun. I've never been so glad to see Bobby Berman's fat cheeks. "Clancy!" he said. "How did you get in there?"

Before I could answer, Monty appeared at his side. She snapped off her skis and climbed down into the pit beside me. "What do you think's broken?" she asked.

I must have looked pretty mangled, because she sounded like *she* was ready to start crying, too. "Nothing's broken," I said. "I'm not even hurt. I'm crying because I'm relieved. I thought I'd be stuck in this hole all day. The bozo that named this trail Child's Play ought to have his head examined!"

Monty stopped digging and looked up in surprise. "This trail is Child's Play?" she exclaimed in amazement. She reached into her pocket and pulled out a trail map. "You're not on Child's Play, Kate," she said after a moment's study. "That's the first trail that branches off Baby Way back there. This is an expert slope."

I pointed up the mountain. "But the sign!" I said.

Bobby and Monty stared at me. All at once I knew what had happened. No accident had sent me onto the wrong slope. The signs on the trails had been purposely switched. The prankster had struck again. And I'd just skied down Death Valley Run.

20

Lars had been right about my bindings being too tight. When Bobby and Monty dug me out, my skis were still firmly clamped onto my feet. They had to unsnap the bindings so I could clamber up out of the pit. When they'd finally unearthed my skis, Monty wanted to race ahead down the hill and send a ski-patrol toboggan up for me, but I said I wanted to ski the rest of the way down under my own power. I know this sounds totally out of character, but I was so nervous about the vicious Snowshoe practical joker, I was sure he'd be the very one to head up my rescue party. With my luck, I'd end up being tobogganed right off the wrong side of the mountain!

Bobby was laboriously dragging two long sticks over to the edge of my pit. He planted them in the snow in the shape of a big, ominous X, to serve as a warning to other skiers. Meanwhile Monty helped me fight my usual battle with my skis. At last, we started down the mountain.

Monty and Bobby took turns staying beside me, though I knew it was painful for them to ski at my tortoise's pace and watch me try to keep my balance. As we went along, they explained how they'd happened to find me. Their class had been canceled because of Pixie's broken leg, so they'd decided to take some runs on their own. When they had come to the top of Death Valley Run, they'd heard my cries and come down to investigate. Actually, they admitted, they'd thought I was a wounded baby mountain goat, baaing for its mother.

"Anyway, this latest trick fits right in with what we were saying last night, Kate," Monty called over her shoulder as we skied. (Despite her valiant efforts, she couldn't help getting a mile ahead of me.) "The Snowshoe screwball is going off the deep end, trying to mess things up around here. Switching trail signs! What a mean thing to do! And dangerous besides."

"You're telling me!" I gasped, struggling to keep from toppling over. "But at least this dirty trick tells us a little bit more about our perpetrator. It has to be someone who's a pretty good skier, to be able to ski and carry trail signs at the same time."

"And also," Monty mused, "it has to be someone who could operate the chair lift by himself, so he could get up the hill without arousing suspicion."

"But Monty, that doesn't really narrow the field at all! Almost everyone on our list is a good skier—and except for Ralph and Nita Nickerson, everyone else is on the hotel staff. They're probably *trained* to run the chair lift!"

Monty and I simultaneously sighed in frustration. As she skied and I wobbled on down the hill, we continued to speculate about the vandal until we'd just about reached the base of the mountain. When we came up to the lodge, I recognized Lars, standing by one of the ski racks. He was peering anxiously up at the trail and compulsively fiddling with the medals around his neck. When he saw me, he started skiing toward me at top speed. Close up I observed that his eye was twitching more furiously than ever.

"Kate!" he cried. "Where have you been? After the whole class made it down Sunny Slope, we waited for you to come out of the ski shop. When you did not emerge, I went in to check, and they said you had never arrived! I was about to find Camille and ask her to order a search of the mountain."

As Monty started to tell him what had happened, a breathless Pixie hobbled out onto the snow on her crutches, closely followed by Peter and Marsha Shade. Then Annie and Nita Nickerson rushed up. Even Ralph Nickerson appeared on the scene. Apparently Lars really *had* sounded the alarm about my failure to appear. When he heard about the trail signs being switched, he looked like he wanted to cry. But was his concern really genuine? I mean, he was the one who'd told me how to get down the hill. Had he known he was sending me to meet my fate on Death Valley Run?

I didn't want to believe it, particularly when he turned to me and clasped my hand. "I am so sorry, Kate. I feel responsible for your having such a bad fright. I will try to think of a way to make it up to you."

His warm words brought sudden tears to my eyes. I'm always a sucker for sympathy, particularly when it's directed at me. And even with their twitch, those Swedish eyes really were an enthralling shade of blue. Since I'd already abandoned my hopeless infatuation for Peter, maybe I could start cultivating a hopeless infatuation for Lars instead.

When Lars left, I stood where I was, staring after him and wondering what to think. The rest of the crowd had also broken up. Pixie had given me a sympathetic smile, and Ralph Nickerson had slapped me on the back and said, "All's well that end's well!" He seemed to have completely forgotten our encounter in the front parlor after the avalanche. Peter Shade had taken a tentative step in my direction, as if he wanted to say something to me, but his mother spoke sharply to him and he turned away.

Naturally, after everyone was gone, I decided I was too shaky to go back up the hill that morning. I bent down to unsnap my bindings, and when I looked up, I saw that Monty was lingering beside me. I asked her what she thought she was doing.

"I've appointed myself your bodyguard," she said. "It's obvious you can't be left alone for a minute." Her tone was joking, but I could tell I'd given her a bad scare up there in my snow pit.

"Look," I said, "I'm going to go into the rental shop and get my bindings adjusted. Then I'm going to go sit by the fire in the parlor and have a cup of hot chocolate. Then I'm going to go into the dining room and grab a good seat for lunch. I know it sounds pretty risky. But I think I can handle it."

She still didn't want to abandon me, and it took all my powers to persuade her to leave me alone. I finally succeeded, however. With a sigh of relief I watched her ski off to join her class. For a while, at least, I needed to be alone with my jumpy nerves.

I carried my skis inside and dropped them off at the rental area, where the man promised to readjust the bindings. On my way out I passed the ski shop and decided that fondling the unbelievably expensive sweaters would be the perfect activity to take my mind off my frightening experience. I opened the door and came face to face with Lynda Dalton, who apparently was the only person in Utah who wasn't aware I'd been missing. As you might expect, she was scrutinizing the makeup display on top of a glass counter.

"Hi, Kathy!" she said cheerily. "When you dropped out of class this morning, I decided to do the same thing. Though I do think Lars is totally cute. Do you think he likes me?"

A nasty, sarcastic remark was trying to fight its way out from between my clenched teeth, and I told myself I'd better leave before I decked Lynda right there between the stretch pants and the après-ski boots. I decided I'd definitely earned at least two cups of hot chocolate, so I went upstairs to the dining room and poured myself a cup from the pot.

It was still pretty early for lunch, so there weren't many people around the lodge yet. Clutching my warm, comforting mug, I wandered across the lobby and into the front parlor. A fire was roaring in the wood-burning stove, and I headed for a snuggly chair right next to it. But before I sat down, I went over to the French windows and looked out. Interesting, I thought. Since the lodge was built on a slope, it was only a very short drop from this room to the ground. It would be quite easy for an athletic person (unlike myself, for example) to climb in or out of the parlor through one of these windows, which incidentally faced in the same direction as the ladies' room in the basement. *Padda, padda, padda*, I thought. Who had it been?

The list of suspects was long, confusing, and frustrating, and I didn't want to think about any of them anymore. I sipped my hot chocolate, sank into a chair, and yawned. After my experience on Death Valley Run, I felt I deserved to be inside, where it was warm and cozy. Someone else could solve the mystery. I was too wrung out to care.

From under my heavy lids I gazed out the French windows, which overlooked a forest bordering an intermediate trail named Robin's Chute. When I allowed myself not to dwell on mystery and danger and malicious pranks, I could appreciate that it was a lovely, peaceful view. Zzzzzz . . . What was that? All at once I sat up straight in my chair. A man on snowshoes was walking through the woods. A ray of bright sunshine bounced off his bald, froggy pate, and I knew it had to be Ted Tedley.

In itself that wasn't so amazing. The man seemed to spend more time at Snowshoe than he did at his own lodge. But I was curious about some long, sticklike things he was dragging along. I couldn't tell what they were, though they appeared too big to be skis.

Grogginess forgotten, I got up again and went to the window for a better look. Then I gasped out loud and sloshed hot chocolate all over my sweater. I'd just figured out what Ted Tedley was carrying. It was a bunch of Snowshoe Mountain trail signs.

21

I was sure I'd caught the would-be poltergeist red-handed. I whirled away from the window and started to run out of the parlor. I didn't know where Camille was. But if I could catch the hotel owner in time, I could show her what Ted Tedley was up to before he hid the evidence of his crime.

I'd just reached the parlor door when Bobby came in. "We have to find Camille," I said. "I think I've caught the prankster!"

Bobby still had his bulky ski boots on, so he couldn't run as fast as I could in my regular shoes. But he puffed along manfully beside me. We met Camille just outside the lodge.

"Camille!" I called to her. "We have to talk to you."

The dark-haired woman smiled, and I stopped in my tracks. For the first time since I'd arrived at Snowshoe, the hotel owner was looking truly happy. Her dark eyes were sparkling as brightly as the jangling bracelets on her wrist and the shiny ring on her left hand. Wow! I thought. At last I'm meeting the real Camille.

"I know what you want, Kate," she said to me. "And I am happy to be able to reassure you. The missing chocolate has mysteriously reappeared. We shall have the torte tonight!"

At any other time this news would have made me ecstatic, but I was too excited about crime busting to start drooling now. "Camille, I *saw* him!" I said. "Ted Tedley! With a bunch of trail signs under his arm!"

Camille shook her head and sighed. "I know," she said. "He carried up a load of supplies for us early this morning. To his surprise he found that the chair lift was running, but there was no one there to operate it! A few days ago he might have thought it was the fault of our ghost, but fortunately, thanks to *you,* Kate, no one accepts that silly idea any longer. Anyway, Ted rode the chair up to the top, where he discovered the trail signs had been rearranged. All of them had been scattered over the mountainside! Luckily, Ted discovered the situation before any of the skiers became confused. This sign rearrangement could have caused a serious accident! It would have been a terrible thing to happen on such a beautiful day!"

You're telling me, I thought, still confused by Camille's sudden good humor. I felt cheated. I'd been envisioning the headlines in the *Skier's Gazette*: Star Eyewitness Puts Finger on Snowshoe Vandal. And now I was hearing that Ted Tedley had actually been helping Camille, bringing up supplies so she could feed her guests, and undoing the vandal's work before it could cause any harm.

The man was almost too good to be true. Why was he so interested in helping Camille solve her problems at the lodge? Maybe all this kindly-neighbor routine was actually an elaborate cover-up for his real activities. After all, he'd conveniently forgotten to fix the mixed-up signs on my trails. Had that really been an oversight on his part? And besides, Camille hadn't seen him marching boldly across the lobby at one A.M. this morning. Maybe she wouldn't feel quite so grateful to Mr. Tedley if she knew about that!

22

I considered telling Camille my theories about Ted Tedley, but she said she had to hurry inside and help prepare lunch. Bobby wanted to go to his room to treat his goggles with defogger spray, so I was on my own again. Nursing an aggrieved, letdown feeling, I wandered back into the lodge.

In the lobby I ran into Nita Nickerson, and was struck once again by how tiny she was. When she stood next to me, she barely came up to my chin. We were a little early for lunch, so we sat down at an empty table to wait. The changeable Ralph had vanished once again, so I decided I might as well try my hand at asking Nita a few subtle questions.

"So Nita," I said casually, "how did you and Ralph pick Snowshoe as the place for your first skiing trip?"

"He talked me into it," she said. Her voice was so bitter, I gave a start of surprise. "If I'd known what it was going to involve—" She broke off abruptly and gave me a sharp look. Then she laughed. "Oh, we've been planning this trip for a long time," she said in her regular kindly tones. "I think I'm just a little too old to learn how to ski for the first time."

Weird. Both the Nickersons seemed to be prone to sudden, dramatic personality changes. I decided to try a new subject. "I wondered if I could ask you an insurance question, Nita," I said. "You see, my father just started this plastic-bracelet business, and while it's doing very well now, he's not sure it always will, public taste being as fickle as it is, and he was thinking of taking out insurance in case his business ever failed, and I was just trying to find out if there is such a thing, and . . ."

I stopped weaving this web of deceit when I realized Nita was barely listening to me. She laughed again and patted my hand. "I don't think anything about insurance, Kate, dear," she said, pushing back her chair. "Why don't I just go get us two cups of hot chocolate to tide us over till lunch?"

I nodded and said sure, even though I'd just had a cup of hot chocolate in the front parlor. Nita headed toward the kitchen, and I stared after her, more convinced than ever that she and Ralph were trying to pull off some kind of charade. After all, she'd just claimed not to know anything about insurance, after having supposedly been married to an insurance salesman for forty years!

As I watched Nita carrying two mugs of hot chocolate back to our table, a disturbing thought came to me. Maybe Nita was the practical joker! She was certainly tiny enough to fit into my wardrobe. Maybe she was an amnesia victim and wasn't always responsible for her actions. Maybe that's why Ralph had been so eager to find out what I'd seen the night of the avalanche. He'd been wondering if I'd seen his wife outside setting off a cannon. And fearing I'd try to have her locked up in an insane asylum for life.

You're probably thinking my imagination was running wild, and that *I* should be locked up in an insane asylum, but I was convinced beyond a shadow of a doubt that I smelled something fishy—and it wasn't lunch, because they'd just started bringing out platters loaded with three-inch-thick, medium-rare bacon cheeseburgers. I'd just picked out a burger and was lovingly decorating it with ketchup and pickles when I saw Lars and Annie beckoning me from the doorway of the dining room. With a wistful look at my plate, I got up and went over to meet them.

"We have just realized what should be done to help you recover from your bad experience this morning," Lars said. "I will give the two of you a private lesson now, free of charge. It will help you get your confidence back."

Don't go, a voice whispered to me. Startled, I glanced over my shoulder and then realized the voice had come from within my own brain.

"I don't know, Lars . . ." I began. "I was thinking of taking the rest of the day off—"

"Oh, please, Kate!" Annie begged. "We missed our lesson this morning, and I was just getting the hang of making parallel turns. If we had a private lesson, we could really learn fast. And we'd never be able to afford it otherwise!"

My friend's little freckled face was so pleading, I felt like a real jerk. Besides, if there were two of us in the lesson, we'd probably be safe. And anyway, Lars's eyes were a divine shade of blue. "I guess we could go up for a while," I said. "After lunch."

"When you are ready," Lars said, "I'll be in the front parlor."

Annie grabbed my arm and started dragging me into the dining room, babbling with excitement about our private lesson with Lars. When had she become such a gung-ho skier? I was about to comment on her newfound enthusiasm, positive she'd fallen for Lars's blue eyes as well as his ski instruction, when Bobby came up, closely followed by Monty and Peter and Marsha Shade. The whole gang of us trooped back into the dining room and sat down with Nita.

I was touched to see that in a motherly gesture, the white-haired woman had covered my cheeseburger with another plate so that it wouldn't get cold. She might be criminally insane, but sometimes she reminded me of my grandma Irene from New Jersey.

As I bit into my juicy burger, I took some time to observe the other people at the table. Bobby was his usual giant Puffbear self, booming away about the great snow conditions on the hill. Monty was also chattering away about the morning's skiing. But Marsha and Peter were maintaining their usual tense silence.

Nita finished her burger and excused herself from the table. I knew I should find a chance to tell Monty and Bobby about my strange conversation with her, but there didn't seem to be much urgency about it. Anyway, it was hard to imagine elderly Nita, who could barely stand up on her skis after two months of lessons, setting off a cannon, *padda padda*ing over the top of the snow, and clambering into the lodge through the parlor windows.

I took another bite of burger and decided not even to think about the "caper" for a while. Often, in my mystery books, the private investigators solve the crimes when they're thinking about something totally different. I had the sense, even as I munched my lunch, that most of the clues I needed were already somewhere in my head. Maybe if I shoved it all out of my mind and concentrated on something else, inspiration would come to me, and I'd see the pattern.

Then, out of the blue, Peter turned to Monty and asked if she wanted to go down Suicide Run with him again after lunch. Peter's mother made a sort of strangling noise in her throat and stared down at her plate. I knew how she felt. I wanted to scream a warning to my cousin, telling her not to go out alone on the hill with that frightening boy. Even though I'd told Monty about my chilling encounter with Peter, I knew she thought I'd over-dramatized it. Besides, I could tell she really liked him. If she decided to go skiing with him, there was nothing that would change her mind.

For a second, after Peter made his suggestion, Monty hesitated. Then she turned and said she'd been *dying* to have another crack at Suicide. In that instant I looked up and my eyes locked with Marsha Shade's. All at once the bookkeeper and I had something in common. Neither one of us trusted Peter as far as we could throw him.

23

I was so agitated and annoyed with my cousin, I almost didn't enjoy my homemade chocolate–chocolate-chip ice cream. The only good thing, I told myself as I ate my second bowl, was that I would be out on the hill at the same time as Monty, though of course Lars would never take Annie and me to ski on Suicide Run, when we could barely make it past the ski racks. But at least I'd be able to keep an eye on Monty on the chair lift and at the top of the mountain, before we went our separate ways.

As I scanned the dining room, I listened to Peter and Monty cheerfully blathering away about the effects of fog on snow, or some such nonsense, and I concluded my cousin was so enraptured, she must have decided to temporarily abandon her detective ambitions and concentrate on her role as a femme fatale. Before I knew it, they'd gotten up from the table, said good-bye, and started out of the dining room.

I sprang into action. I grabbed Annie's arm and hauled her to her feet. Without explaining my hurry, I dragged her across the lobby and into the parlor, where we found Lars impatiently waiting for us. As we came back out into the lobby, I saw Pixie and Camille having a conversation near the bank of lockers. Camille was frowning, but even so, she didn't look anywhere near as awful as she had two days before.

We passed the lockers, and Pixie started to give me her friendly smile. Then, when she saw Lars and Annie behind me, she gave a little frown, stuffed her tissue into her pocket, and reached for her crutches, which were leaning against the wall. She probably wanted to come over and warn us to play it safe in the fog, but I was in too much of a hurry to wait for her.

When we stepped outside, I understood why Monty and Peter had been talking about fog. Sometime during lunch a fat, gray cloud had come to rest on top of Snowshoe Mountain. I believe "pea soup" is the term commonly used to describe this kind of fog. Since I don't like pea soup, I prefer to think of it as clam chowder.

Monty and Peter already had their skis on and were heading toward the main lift that went up to the top of the mountain. As they waved good-bye to us, I had to peer through the fog to see their faces. Within seconds they were swallowed up by the swirling mist.

Lars was waiting for Annie and me to get our skis on. Finally we were both ready. When we got to the bottom of the main chair lift, Lars started to tell us to get on a chair together, but then, out of nowhere, Nita Nickerson appeared on her child-sized skis, so Lars put Annie on a chair with her, and I won the dubious pleasure of riding up with him.

Amazingly, I got onto the chair without mishap and immediately started worrying about getting off at the top. Lars's pleasantly accented voice broke through my haze of anxiety. "Have your activities as a detective been successful, Kate?" he asked.

I gave a start of surprise. Fortunately, Lars had remembered to lower the safety bar, so I didn't tumble off the chair. "How did you know about that?" I asked.

"Don't you remember? Your friend Bobby told Pixie and me all about it yesterday afternoon. I'm sure the whole ski lodge knows about it by now. Have you learned anything?"

I shot him a sideways glance. He was gazing intently at me with his penetrating, ice-blue eyes. Why, I wondered, was he so interested in our amateur investigations?

He seemed almost to read my mind. "I had hoped, you see," he explained with a little laugh, "that you might stumble upon some kind of clue as to who has been causing all these problems at the lodge—now that we have eliminated the poltergeist idea, that is. Camille is unwilling to call in the police, because she is afraid the guests will not like it. But they already do not like what has been happening, and I have begun to fear that things will not go well for Snowshoe. Camille hired me on a trial basis only, giving me the hope of one day heading up the ski school. But if things do not go well here, my future will surely be affected."

Well, this was a sad story, and I did feel a pang of sympathy. But Lars's voice sounded so disturbed that I felt more uneasy than ever. Had I really been wise to come up on the mountain with him? I'd thought I'd be safe enough with Annie around, but I hadn't reckoned on the fog, and as guard dogs went, Annie was more of a Pekingese than a German shepherd. Plus, even though I *knew* there were skiers in front of us and behind us, our private little chair was in a strangely isolated spot, suspended on a thin cable, swaying high above the ski trail, invisible in the mist.

Before I had time to get myself really spooked, we reached the top of our lift. It was so foggy up there, I could barely see the PREPARE TO UNLOAD sign. Just in time we put up our safety bar, placed our poles in our outside hands, and picked up the tips of our skis.

My dismount was spectacular. It made this morning's dramatic fall with Annie look like nothing. As I pushed forward to stand up and glide down the hill, my body wouldn't budge! I pushed and pushed, but still nothing happened. In a panic, I looked down and saw that my zipper had become wedged in one of the cracks in the chair. I began tugging frantically, sure I was about to be dragged under the chair and crushed against the giant pillar that held up the cable.

My zipper pulled free. I threw myself off the chair and grabbed onto the nearest support I could find, which turned out to be Lars's leg. Lars shouted with surprise. Then my crazily kicking ski landed on top of his, pinning his foot to the ground. The sudden check of his movement caused his arms to shoot straight out into the air and his body to tilt forward at an incredible angle. His bindings released and he flipped into the air and fell down the path.

The lift operator had finally gotten around to stopping the chair, so I had time to pick myself up and ski down to Lars's side. When I got there, Annie and Nita were already helping him get to his feet. He looked a little dazed, as if he didn't quite know where he was. Nita scurried around looking for the hat and gloves that had gone flying during the fall.

"Gosh, Lars," I said. "I'm really sorry. My zipper caught in the chair."

Lars shook his head. "It's all right, Ingrid," he said.

"*Kate*, Lars! It's Kate Clancy!"

The ski instructor blinked, and intelligence slowly returned to the fjordlike eyes. "Ah, yes, of course," he said slowly. "Kate. And Annie. Here for your private lesson."

Nita scuttled through the fog, carrying Lars's hat and gloves. "And look what else I found," she exclaimed, holding out her hand. "Over there by the trail sign. Do they belong to the handyman, do you think? That boy Peter Shade?"

Annie, Lars, and I all leaned forward to peer at the object in Nita's palm. I saw what it was and gasped. The belonging that Nita had recovered was a pair of wire cutters—just the right size for cutting through a bunch of lift tickets.

I remembered Peter's tool belt, and I opened my mouth to say they were probably his. But then I heard Lars speaking. "Those are not Peter's wire cutters," he said. "Those are mine. I must have misplaced them earlier."

The ski instructor moved to take the wire cutters. Suddenly I saw a hand reach out and grab them before Lars's fingers had time to close over them. To my horror, I realized the hand was my own. But I seemed unable to stop it. Still controlled by some outside force, I yanked the clippers away and stuffed them into my pocket. I pushed off with my poles and skied off into the fog. I was going as fast as I could, but I had absolutely no idea where I was headed.

24

As I inched along through the gray haze, one thought kept coming back to me. Without a doubt I had gone absolutely, totally bananas. In my heady excitement at seeing what I thought was a real clue, I'd acted like a reckless fool, snatching those wire cutters like some kind of crazed kleptomaniac. To top it off, instead of staying near Nita and Annie, who might have been able to help me, I'd gone off alone, like a fugitive from a roller derby. And now here I was, pretending I knew how to ski and barely able to see two inches in front of my nose.

I wished I could stop and try to figure out where I was. If I looked at my trail map, I could probably get a pretty good idea. I knew we'd gotten off at the top of the main chair, and to the best of my recollection, I'd taken off toward the left, or west side of the mountain. I stuck my skis out into their widest possible wedge position and turned sideways into the hill to stop. I fumbled in my pocket for my soggy trail map and my fingers touched the cold metal of the pilfered wire cutters. Just then I heard someone calling my name.

Even with the muffling effect of the fog, Lars's Swedish accent was unmistakable. And I could tell he wasn't far behind me. I almost believed I could hear him breathing down my neck. I was more and more convinced he was the prankster and that I was carrying the precious evidence that would send him to the slammer.

I pushed off with my poles and cautiously started down the hill again. Suddenly I remembered that Lars was a former member of the Swedish ski-racing team. I shuddered. With my clumsy, molasses-in-January-style skiing, how did I stand a chance of getting away from a racer, particularly a racer who most likely was insane with rage?

The mountainside was very quiet. The fog seemed to put a damper on all the noise, sort of like the pieces of cotton I stuff in my ears when my father is playing his John Philip Sousa albums. The only thing I could hear was the sound of my two skis scraping against the soft snow. But wait a minute. Was I really hearing only two skis? I held my breath and listened hard. There was definitely another set of skis scraping along off to the right. It sounded like they were only a few yards away!

Lars had obviously caught up with me, but probably couldn't see me in the fog. If I stopped completely, he might actually pass me. I pointed my toes together and tried to go into my wedge. *Boing!* All at once I crashed over a big bump and just about lost my balance. My body was thrown back and then forward again. *Ka-bam!* My neck whiplashed backward and my knees folded up almost to my chest as I bounced up on top of another bump. My legs stretched themselves out again as I plummeted down the other side.

There was something sickeningly familiar about this. It

couldn't be, but I was positive it was. If this trail wasn't Death Valley Run, I'd eat my ski pole.

I gritted my teeth and bent my knees to absorb the shock of the next bump. I'd survived this run once today, and I'd just have to survive it again. At least this time I had some idea of the torment in store for me. By some incredible fluke I went over the next mogul without my usual bone-jarring jolt. But as soon as I'd plunged down into the rutty little valley beyond it, another, bigger mound loomed ahead.

Automatically, I went into a knee hunch as my body traveled up the side of an enormous icy lump. As I turned to the left, I tried to shift my weight to my downhill ski, just as I'd been taught. As usual, the tips of my skis crossed and I tripped. I sat down hard right on top of the biggest mogul on Snowshoe Mountain.

"Kate," Lars said. "At last I have caught you."

"Oh no you have not!" I jerked away from his hand. In a flash I was up—and in another one I'd fallen and was sliding down the trail on my stomach. As I bounced along, I had a sudden inspiration. It would be tricky, but I couldn't think of anything else to try. Once again I could hear the scrape of Lars's skis right behind me.

As soon as I'd come to a stop, I sat up and stared straight ahead of me. I struggled to my feet and tried to walk *across* the trail. I fell down a few times, but at last I saw what I wanted: the row of large evergreen trees that lined the edge of the slope.

Boing! I slid sideways and somersaulted over another

bump. Then I rolled a few times and came to a stop. I brushed the ice globs out of my eyes and sat up. I was looking right at the X Bobby had left to warn skiers away from my snow pit. One way or another, I'd reached my goal.

On my hands and knees I hauled myself, skis and all, over to the sticks. Awkwardly, with my snow-encrusted mittens, I tugged at the X. "Over here, Lars!" I shouted. "I'm over here." I heard the scrape of approaching skis. But I couldn't get the sticks out of the snow!

Lars was coming closer. Desperately, I hauled at the sticks. They still wouldn't budge. *Scccrrape.* One of them began to wobble. I could see Lars now. *Yank!* The stick came up in my hand. The other one fell sideways.

I called Lars's name again. Now I could see his dark shape approaching. He must have seen me as well, because he left the trail and came toward me. He turned his skis to stop by my side, but it was too late. He'd gone just a few feet too far. With a yell of surprise he skied out into thin air. Then he sank deep into the snow of my pit.

I realized I didn't have much time. I couldn't see Lars very well, but I could hear him thrashing and grunting around down in the hole. It had been an effective trap for a puny weakling like me, but an athlete like Lars wouldn't have much trouble digging himself out. My only choice seemed to be to ski (so to speak) down the hill as fast as I could, grab the first skier I saw, and beg for protection.

For a few precious seconds I stood at the edge of the woods, psyching myself into starting down the foggy trail.

Inside my sodden purple mittens, my fingers were freezing. Feverishly, I rubbed them up and down on my legs to warm them up. *Click!* Something connected in a remote part of my brain. Something to do with rubbing fingers. But what? And what did it have to do with getting away from Lars the prankster?

Calm down, you panic-stricken pea brain! my little inner voice said sharply. You're doing just what someone out there wants you to do! You're looking at the obvious clues and assuming Lars is guilty! But if you think about it, you'll realize the wire cutters were either an accident or a plant! You know Lars has a toolbox in his locker. You know he carries tools around with him so he can adjust his equipment. Those wire cutters don't prove a thing. You'd better go back and help him out of that pit.

Ulp. I swallowed hard. I *hate* that nasty little voice. But once again it was making a disturbingly good point. And now it was screaming about something else. Put all the clues together, Kate! it was saying. And you'll have the answer!

"Okay," I said. Mechanically, I continued to rub my fingers as I spoke. "Put all the clues together. If Lars isn't guilty, someone sure is trying to make it look that way. That means the prankster is someone with some kind of grudge against him. But who? The wet footprints point to someone who lives outside the lodge. The—"

Sccrrape. My thoughts were interrupted. I couldn't believe my ears. Another skier had actually chosen to ski on Death Valley Run in this fog. Ignoring a loud inner warning, I moved back out onto the trail. "Help!" I shouted. "Over here!"

The scraping sound abruptly stopped. And then, through the heavy dead silence of the fog, I heard it. The maddeningly familiar, muffled sound I'd heard in my room the night my suitcase had been stolen. Uh-oh.

You stopped thinking too soon, mushbrain! my little voice shouted. It went on: The hiding-in-the-wardrobe trick points to someone small. The mixed-up trail signs point to a good skier. All of it adds up to only one person. And that person is—

But wait! I interrupted myself. That's impossible! That person can't be the one! She couldn't have done it!

Unless, that is, unless . . . Suddenly, my mind shifted into fifth gear, and everything became clear as ice crystals. I realized that rubbing my frozen fingers now was reminding me of rubbing my dirty fingers at dinnertime. In a bright flash of blinding insight, I knew what that flaky white stuff had been. I even figured out where I'd gotten it on my hands. As I gasped at the realization, I heard the familiar muffled sound once again. But this time, with a terrible lurch of my heart, I recognized what it was.

"Pixie," I said out loud. Of course. The sound I'd heard in my room had been a sneeze, suddenly smothered in a wadded-up green tissue. It was unmistakable. But I didn't have time to wonder why I hadn't recognized it sooner. Because now I was face to face with the saboteur of Snowshoe Mountain Lodge.

25

"Plaster," I said out loud. "The white stuff on my hands was plaster from that phony cast of yours. You must have accidentally gotten some onto your clipboard. That's where I got it."

Frosty silence. It should have warned me, but I was too overwhelmed by my discovery to be afraid. "Your leg was never broken at all," I prattled on. "We should have realized you never would have been back from the hospital so fast. You made up that story about someone pushing you off the trail, so everyone would think you'd been a victim. You even hinted it might have been Lars who did it. You planted my scarf and the chocolate and my suitcase in Lars's locker. Why, you must have planted those wire cutters by the trail sign just now!"

Pixie gave a low laugh that was anything but perky. "I had to act fast," she said. "But fortunately it takes you and Annie so long to get your skis on, I had time to get my cast off and take the lift up the hill before you were even ready. I was sure you'd think Lars was guilty."

"I did think that," I breathed softly. "But then I figured out the part about the plaster. And you sneezed, just the way you did the night in my room when you were pretending to be a ghost."

"This stupid cold!" Pixie raged. "It'll be the death of me yet! I'm sure it's psychological. I've had it ever since Camille made me only the *acting* head of the ski school because she thinks I need to improve my teaching techniques—and then I find out she's told Lars Lundquist *he'd* be the head if he had another good season. Lars Lundquist! Why, everyone knows he's crazy as a coot!"

The word "crazy" seemed to hang above us in the heavy, sinister mist. Pixie's face, which I'd always thought was so cute and friendly, was twisted in a gremlinlike snarl of anger and self-pity. As I stared at her, the mixed-up jigsaw-puzzle pieces in my mind began fitting themselves together in a neat, interlocking pattern. I realized that right from the beginning, Pixie had been trying to throw suspicion on other people at the lodge. The first time I'd met her, she'd been complaining about the icy sidewalk—which she'd probably been responsible for! When I'd arrived at the lodge, she'd been the only one who'd seen how much I valued Dad's suitcase, and it had been stolen that same night. Pixie had been limping around the halls right after the chocolate had been pilfered, and her missing clipboard had turned up in the kitchen. She'd been unusually out of breath right after the avalanche had been set, undoubtedly because she'd been running around outside, setting off the cannon. She'd made up the story about her injury and then wondered out loud where Lars had been at the time.

Looking back on it, it was all plain as day. I should have solved the puzzle much earlier. But I didn't have time to think about that now. I had to get out of there. "I think

I'll just ski on down now," I said in what I hoped was a matter-of-fact tone.

"No you won't, Kate." Pixie's voice was as cold and hard as the snowy trail beneath our skis. "You're the only one who knows the truth. If you keep quiet, I can still pin this thing on Lars. He'll be fired, and I'll get his job."

"Oh, I'll be quiet, Pixie," I promised.

"I'm afraid I can't take that chance."

Uh-oh. Where was my bossy, all-knowing inner voice when I really needed it? I seemed to be completely on my own, with a person who hadn't hesitated to start a danger-ous avalanche!

I had to get out of there. *Now.* In a desperate attempt at escape, I started to push off with my poles. Pixie put out a hand to stop me, and I pushed harder. Naturally, this caused me to lose my ever-precarious balance and topple over. Fortunately, however, I fell forward, and knocked tiny Pixie to the ground. Her leg twisted sideways and her binding released. As her right ski fell off, she cursed loudly.

Amazingly, I managed to get to my feet and push off down the hill before Pixie could get her ski back on. But within a minute I heard the familiar scrape of another skier speeding along right behind me. Pixie was hot on my wedged-out heels.

Sproing! I bounced over one last bump and fell down. As I struggled up again, I wondered how much more of this abuse my poor body could take. Fortunately, I remem-bered from this morning that the trail would level off soon. Then there would only be a few hundred yards to the bottom of the hill. If the fog continued to hide me, I'd be home free. If Pixie didn't get me first.

Pixie. Sweet, pigtailed Pixie. Would anyone believe me? I bitterly remembered how I'd leaped to her defense when Monty had suggested her as a suspect. She was too sweet, I'd argued. Too nice. But it had all been an act!

I passed by another bump, and then I was inchworming along on smooth snow. It couldn't be much farther now. I stared ahead, trying to locate the lodge buildings at the bottom of the trail. But the fog made it impossible to see much of anything. On the one hand that was a help, because it meant Pixie couldn't see me. But on the other hand, what was to stop me from skiing right into the side of a bus on the parking lot?

The scrootch of Pixie's skis was getting louder and louder. At any moment I expected her to leap onto my back and strangle me with her strong little hands. I prayed I was near the bottom. I felt like I was skiing through swirls of wet, gray cotton candy. It was taking so long to get down, I was beginning to be afraid I'd accidentally left the main trail and skied off onto the side trail that connected with one of the little-used chair lifts. If I had, it meant disaster, because that area would almost certainly be deserted in this weather. And I was sure Pixie would know it like the back of her hand.

There was nothing to tell me where I was. Nothing, that is, except for that distant booming sound, whatever it might be. I listened hard and steered myself in that direction. Then, despite my fear, I started to smile. All at once I laughed out loud. I'd just realized what the booming sound was.

I will never call Bobby Berman "Mouth" again. But I might call him Foghorn. Because that was the job he did for me that afternoon. For the rest of my days I'll be grateful for his loud voice.

At last I could see buildings and people in front of me. I was so excited, I abandoned my beloved wedge position and went into what racers call a "tuck," pointing straight down the hill, with my body curled up like a deep-fat-fried shrimp. Of course, by the time I reached the bottom, I was going so fast I was completely out of control. With a clash of skis and poles, I smacked into the side of the lift-ticket office.

Suddenly I was surrounded by people. First Camille and Ted Tedley came out of the lodge and ran to my side. Bobby and Annie hurried over from the ski racks, and Peter and Monty appeared out of nowhere. They still had their skis on, so they'd probably just come down the hill.

"What's going on?" Monty asked. "We just saw Pixie skiing down toward the parking lot. What happened to her broken leg?"

"It was a fake!" I managed to gasp out. "Someone has to stop her!"

Another skier zipped by and shot down the little hill toward the parking lot. I blinked and did a double take. The skier was Ralph Nickerson, the retired insurance salesman who'd made such a show of being the clumsiest clod in the beginners' class. But just now he'd looked like a World Cup champion!

"Do not worry," Camille said softly. "I think he will catch her. In his job, they are trained to capture the fugitives."

"Insurance salesmen are trained to capture fugitives?" Annie asked in confusion.

"Oh, no, Annie," said Camille. "He is not an insurance salesman. He is a private detective."

Aha. My phoniness detector had been right on the button. Ralph Nickerson was a faker. But fortunately for all of us, he was still a good guy.

As I struggled to my feet, Annie gave a little scream. "What is that?" she cried. We all turned to look in the direction she was pointing. Something was approaching us from out of the fog. It was big and white, and it seemed to be gliding along without touching the ground.

Annie screamed again, and everyone else gasped. I'm sure they all thought the Abominable Snowman had just come down from the top of Snowshoe Mountain. I, of course, knew better. I realized that poor innocent Lars had finally managed to dig himself out of my snow pit. And now I was sure he was ready to kill me.

26

Two hours later we were all dressed in dry clothes and drowning our memories in hot chocolate in the parlor. As the heroine of the day, I'd nabbed the most comfortable squashy chair right in front of the fireplace. Bobby, Annie, Peter, and Monty were sprawled out on pillows on the floor, while the older set—Camille, Ted Tedley, Nita, and Marsha Shade—were sitting on some of the folding chairs we used for watching the movies. Even Lars was there, still shivering under several layers of blankets. His lips were now a perfect color match for his beautiful blue eyes.

An outsider looking in through one of the French windows might have thought the bunch of us formed a cozy scene, that we were a family of contented, pleasantly weary ski bunnies, warming our tails by the fire after a hard day on the slopes. But as you know, that would have been a few hops shy of the truth.

I just couldn't get rid of the image of Pixie's face. After Ralph Nickerson had pursued her down to the parking lot, we'd all scrambled along behind him to see if we could help. When we'd arrived at the top of the wooden steps, we'd seen Pixie standing with her back up against someone's sleek silver-gray BMW. Slowly, Ralph had walked toward her. At first Pixie had tried to put on her perky act again and argue that she was innocent. But when she'd realized no one believed her and that she was really caught, she revealed her true feelings to everyone.

"Six years!" she'd said. "I worked here for six years. I should have been head of the ski school for life! This stupid lodge doesn't deserve to exist!"

As Ralph had approached Pixie from the front, petite Nita Nickerson had materialized in the fog right behind the silver car. The older woman had put a hand on the redhead's arm and said a few words in a low voice. Pixie had closed her mouth and obediently allowed Nita to guide her into the backseat of the car. Fortunately, the fancy BMW had turned out to belong to the Nickersons, so it had been an easy matter for the two of them to drive Pixie to the police station.

And now, here we all were, sitting in the parlor, listening to Ralph, who had just returned.

"I'm still not clear," Marsha Shade was saying, "on why Pixie was trying to put the lodge out of business."

Ralph started to answer, but before he got a word out, Bobby took over. "Frustrated ambition," he boomed authoritatively. "If she couldn't be head of the ski school, she'd ruin the lodge!"

Camille shook her head sadly, and I almost expected to see her pull a pill bottle out of her pocket. Instead, though, she fondled a shining ring on her left hand. "I had no idea she was so upset," she said. "I had told her many times that she needed to work on her teaching technique. She seemed to accept what I was saying. But all the time she must have been burning inside. To think she went to all that trouble of faking a broken leg."

"It was a master stroke," Ralph admitted. "It kept me from suspecting her of being the prankster."

Marsha Shade laughed a too-loud laugh. "You won't believe this," she said brightly, "but for a little while there I actually thought Peter was responsible for all the pranks. I know it sounds outrageous, but I had the silliest idea that he thought that the only way I'd let him join the pro racing circuit was if he made me lose my job here and we became desperate for money!" She turned to Peter, patted him on the arm, and smiled brightly. "I'm sorry, dear. But after all, you did try to drop out of school last year, and . . . somehow, through her little tricks, Pixie managed to get all of us acting crazy. I even went so far as to tell Camille I'd seen the ghost. I thought it would keep her from suspecting Peter."

"That's okay, Mom," Peter said. "I thought *you* were the prankster. I thought you might have been embezzling money so you could send me off to one of those fancy private colleges you're always talking about, and that you decided to ruin Snowshoe before you got caught!" He turned to me and favored me with his slightly wicked smile. "That's why I was so upset with you the other night, Kate, when I found you spying. I thought you were about to catch my mother in the act of juggling the books."

After the Shade family-confession session, Ralph seized the floor again. "At the station," he began, "Pixie told us everything. It seems that when Camille took over the lodge last year and started making changes, Pixie assumed she'd be made head of the ski school when the former head retired. But when she was named the *acting* head, she devised the plan of bringing the lodge to its knees through all these acts of sabotage. Given the gloomy atmosphere of this place, the ghostly legend idea was a natural. She decided to plant the story of a spook and harass the guests till Snowshoe got such a terrible reputation, Camille would have to close down. But then Pixie heard that if Lars had another great season like he had last year, the ski-school job would be his. About the same time, Kate here figured out the solution to all the locked-room puzzles Pixie had been relying on to support her ghost theory. So—"

"So," Bobby broke in, "Pixie decided to abandon the ghost plan and frame Lars as the prankster instead! She thought that with his mental history, everyone would think he'd cracked up. In fact, she decided that would be an improvement over her original plan, because if Lars took the rap for the sabotage, she might end up with his job after all!"

Ralph shot Bobby a bitter look, and I felt a pang of sympathy for the detective. Two months of undercover work, only to have his best theatrical moment swiped clean away.

Lars shook his blond head sadly. A few drops of melted snow flew out of his hair and landed on the rug. "I had no idea Pixie had it in for me," he said. "I thought . . . I was afraid I might be having another breakdown. Doing things without realizing it. Thank goodness it wasn't true."

As he spoke, there was no sign of either a twitch or a medal fiddle.

"There's one thing I still haven't worked out," I said. "All this business about the wire cutters. First Peter loses his tool belt, but then it reappears in his room. Then Pixie plants Lars's wire cutters at the top of the chair lift. It doesn't make sense!"

"Pixie explained that down at the station," Ralph said. "She got the idea for clipping the ticket wires when she saw Peter's belt hanging on the hook on the desk in the lobby. She grabbed the whole belt and waited for her chance, which came after lunch. But since she wanted to frame Lars for the job, she returned Peter's belt to his room, stole Lars's wire cutters from his locker, and later put the wire cutters up by the trail sign in a very obvious spot."

Annie smiled up at Nita. "What's it like being married to a private detective?" she asked.

Nita smiled thoughtfully. "Oh, well, I've never paid much attention to Ralph's work up till now," she said. "This was the first time he brought me in on a job, to help out with his 'cover,' as he calls it." She nodded and patted her husband's hand. "But after this afternoon I believe I have a natural flare for this business. I think I just might help out more often!"

"You and Ralph both helped us out a lot," Camille said to her. "And to think I almost didn't hire you because I believed our problem was ghosts. But Ted insisted I bring in a detective, just in case." She beamed at the squat

163

figure beside her. "I might as well tell you all now," she said, "that Ted and I decided this afternoon to become engaged."

Well, that explained Camille's sudden happiness in the midst of chaos this afternoon. But I still had my doubts about her froggy fiancé. Before I knew it, I twisted around to face Ted and asked, "What were you doing snooping around the hotel here last night? We saw you come into the lobby."

Ted blinked his buggy eyes, and I almost expected to see his tongue flick out and capture a fly. Instead, he smiled. "I was just keeping an eye on things," he said heartily. "I'd fallen into the habit of making routine checks on the lodge, about six P.M. and one A.M. every night." I remembered the squat shadowy shape I'd seen outside Bobby's and my windows the first night I'd arrived.

"Since Ted professed his love for me several months ago," Camille added, "my problems have become his. Even though he convinced me to hire Ralph, he still was very anxious about our safety here. And also, he has been working late hours to help poor Marsha figure out how we can best merge our business interests." Another piece of the puzzle fell into place: the reason why Marsha had been working in the office in the wee hours of the morning.

As Ted and Camille continued to beam at one another, I carefully avoided looking at Monty. We'd spent the last two days making amphibian jokes about Ted Tedley, only to learn that attractive, intelligent Camille was planning to marry him! I guess it just goes to prove that one person's frog is another person's prince.

"Wait a minute," Peter Shade said. "How did you know my tool belt reappeared in my room, Kate?"

My face turned bright red. On the floor beside me Monty tensed her muscles, ready to spring at my throat for revealing that we'd snooped around in Peter's room. I cleared my throat and started stammering a feeble explanation when, to my amazement and relief, Bobby spoke up.

"You were a suspect, Shade," he said abruptly. "Everyone was. Your door was open, and I went in and searched your room." Bobby has a slight tendency to hog credit for himself. Still, in this case, it was noble of him to leave Monty and me out of it. The detectives' handbook probably has some kind of rule about protecting broads.

For another fifteen minutes or so everyone talked on and on about the case. I talked right along with them until my stomach began making louder noises than my voice box. At last Camille looked at her watch and exclaimed that she should have been at work in the kitchen long ago. We could hear other guests passing through the lobby en route to the dining room, so we all got up and hurried to join the stampede. On the way I noticed Lynda Dalton holding hands with Darwin from Valley High. If you ask me, Computa-Date couldn't have come up with a more perfectly paired couple.

I'll try to restrain myself when I describe that night's dinner, except to say it was the best yet. I *will* tell you that we finally got to have the chocolate mousse torte for dessert, and that I could wax poetic about every mouthful.

Anyway, the rest of the ski week wasn't bad either. I really made a lot of progress with my skiing. Lars kept on teaching the beginners. What a man. Not only did he spare my humble life, but he even went so far as to say he "understood" why I'd trapped him in the snow pit. Still, I did notice he didn't offer to give me another private lesson. . . .

Marsha Shade took a break from the books and took over Peter's intermediate ski class, and Peter started teaching the experts, which meant that he and Monty got to ski together all morning. She and Bobby and Annie and I still skied together every afternoon, though, and we all had a great time getting hysterical every time I fell down.

Throughout the entire week my cool-as-a-cucumber cousin put on a slick show of pretending she didn't really care about Peter Shade. She may have had the ridiculous notion that *I* had a crush on him and been trying to spare my feelings. Whatever her reasons were, she didn't fool me. When the last day of the vacation finally arrived, she ran into the bathroom and blew her nose at least four hundred times. With Monty, that passes for a violent emotional scene. I wished I could have comforted her somehow, but I know she likes to handle these things on her own.

Actually, I felt pretty bad myself when it came time to say good-bye to Lars and Camille and everyone. When Monty pressed a farewell bag of peanut M&M's into my hand, I started sniveling all over the parking lot. I knew we'd see each other again next summer, but just then, standing there in the grimy snow, summer seemed like an eternity away.

Still, in the friends department, I'd come away from Snowshoe with more than I'd had when I'd arrived. First of all there was Annie, my sister from the slopes. It turned out she didn't live very far from me at home, so besides seeing each other at Pacifico, we'd be able to get together after school and on weekends. Also, I guess you'd have to count Lynda Dalton as a new chum, even if she did still think my name was Kathy. And then, of course, there's Bobby Berman. True, he's still as loud and bossy as ever. But now I know that under that chubby exterior there lives a really decent friend.

In spite of everything that happened, I was glad I'd gone skiing. After all, I'd gotten to see Monty, I'd made some new friends, I'd lost in love—twice—and I'd helped solve a real mystery.

Given the chance, I think I'll go skiing again. Of course, it's not likely I'll get the chance anytime soon. When my parents hear the true tale of the Mystery at Snowshoe Mountain Lodge, they'll lock me in the house for the next two hundred years. But that's a whole other story. . . .